QUO VADIS, BABY?

Quo Vadis, Baby?

by

Grazia Verasani

◎◉◎◉

Translated by

Taylor Corse and Juliann Vitullo

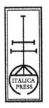

ITALICA PRESS
NEW YORK
2018

Italian Original
Quo Vadis, Baby?
© 2004 Arnoldo Mondadori Editore S.p.A., Milano
under exclusive license with Colorado Noir

Translation Copyright © 2017,
Taylor Corse and Juliann Vitullo

Italica Press Modern Italian Fiction Series

ITALICA PRESS, INC.
595 Main Street, Suite 605
New York, New York 10044

Library of Congress Cataloging-in-Publication Data
Names: Verasani, Grazia, author. | Corse, Taylor, 1951- translator. |
  Vitullo, Juliann M., translator.
Title: Quo vadis, baby? / by Grazia Verasani ; translated by Taylor Corse and
  Juliann Vitullo.
Description: New York : Italica Press, 2017. | Series: Italica Press modern
  Italian fiction series
Identifiers: LCCN 2017027425 (print) | LCCN 2017028841 (ebook) | ISBN
  9781599103679 (ebook) | ISBN 9781599103655 (hardcover : alk. paper) |
  ISBN 9781599103662 (pbk. : alk. paper)
Subjects: LCSH: Women private investigators--Italy--Fiction. | Bologna
  (Italy)--Fiction. | Mystery fiction.
Classification: LCC PQ4922.E64 (ebook) | LCC PQ4922.E64 Q613 2017
  (print) |
  DDC 853/.92--dc23
LC record available at https://lccn.loc.gov/2017027425

Cover Image: Piazza Maggiore, Bologna. Photo © Italica Press Archive.

For a Complete List of
Modern Italian Fiction
Visit our Web Site at
http://www.italicapress.com/index011.html

ABOUT THE TRANSLATORS

TAYLOR CORSE is an associate professor of English at Arizona State University. Professor Corse has written extensively about the literary culture of seventeenth- and eighteenth-century England, including such writers as John Dryden, Aphra Behn, Anne Conway, Alexander Pope, and Tobias Smollett. He has also translated works from Latin and Italian, most recently the selected poetry of Ferruccio Benzoni.

JULIANN VITULLO IS an associate professor of Italian at the School of International Letters and Cultures at Arizona State University where she also served as Associate Director. She has written on various aspects of medieval, early modern, and contemporary Italian culture with emphasis on the relationship between literary traditions and the material world, including economics, food, and gender studies.

INTRODUCTION

Playwright, musician, singer, composer, and author of several novels, including her debut work of crime fiction — *Quo Vadis, Baby?*— Grazia Verasani is a versatile and accomplished artist. Originally published in 2004, *Quo Vadis, Baby?* is the first of five novels that feature Giorgia Cantini, a female private detective who lives and works in Bologna, Italy. Over the years, *QVB* has attracted readers throughout Italy and the rest of Europe. In 2005, Gabriele Salvatores produced an excellent film version of the novel, which in turn inspired a popular TV mini-series on Sky Cinema. For all this commercial and critical success, no English-language version of *QVB* has been available until now.

At first glance, Giorgia is not a pretty sight. She is sitting at a bar, downing her fourth cocktail of the night (a gin bitter, her signature drink); feeling moody and obnoxious, she quarrels with a stranger who knocks her to the ground. What is bothering Giorgia? Apparently, it is a cache of letters from her long-dead sister, which has just come to light. This stirs up a host of painful memories. Too drunk to drive, Giorgia nevertheless gets behind the wheel of her battered Citroën and makes her way to the cemetery where her sister Ada and her mother are buried. There she finds Ada's grave and recalls an awkward conversation the two of them had at her mother's funeral. Right from the outset, this novel announces that it is more concerned with character and family history than it is with traditional sleuthing. Moreover, it is always within the framework of intimate, everyday relationships, at home and in the office, that Verasani locates larger social tensions and conflicts.

In these opening pages, Verasani also sets the distinctive tone and style for her remarkable novel. She writes concisely and vividly, interspersing brief vignettes with taut dialogue and spare description. Giorgia Cantini, her protagonist–narrator, dominates the fictional world of *QVB*, and we learn lots about her personal likes (she is fond of eighties punk rock and bohemian counter-culture) and dislikes (she despises the slick and sleek businessmen of urban Bologna). She cares very little about her personal appearance, wearing the same drab green trousers and military flight jacket to work every day. She smokes too much, exercises too little, eats on the run, and — the cardinal sin for Italian women — is a messy housekeeper. Noted for her brutal honesty, she is not afraid to speak her mind to clients, friends, police officers, or complete strangers. Despite, or perhaps because of, these prickly traits, people are drawn to Giorgia. Men want to have sex with her, even though she is not seductive or traditionally feminine. (She turns down some offers and accepts others.) Clients confide in her about their fears and worries, which mainly have to do with unfaithful partners and spouses. Unmarried and uninterested in marriage, she investigates the tangled affairs of unhappily married people. She is a loner, like so many fictional detectives, but unlike most of her counterparts, she is enmeshed in a web of personal relationships. This is perhaps her most endearing quality. Giorgia befriends all sorts of unlikely people — Lucio, the gay IT consultant who shares her offices; Mel, vinyl merchant who shares her tastes in music; Gigi, the jazz pianist who shares her bed from time to time; and most surprising of all, Gaia, the "goth" teenage girl with a taste for poetry who — like Giorgia — has had more than her share of family misery.

Giorgia's most difficult relationship is with her alcoholic father, Fulvio Cantini, retired major of the carabinieri and nominal head of the Cantini Detective Agency. Although Giorgia runs the office and handles all the cases, Fulvio still pops in from time to time to check up on his daughter and dispense unwanted advice. She bristles when he criticizes the way she manages the business, but she neither confronts nor contradicts him. The Major is secretly pleased by Giorgia's competence and efficiency, but he cannot bring himself to admit it. Later on, when she does question her father about the murky circumstances surrounding her sister's suicide, this becomes one of Giorgia's break-through moments. Conflicted relationships also persist with other family members, chiefly with Ada, the beloved and much troubled older sister, whose ghostly presence haunts the novel from beginning to end.

Wary of romance, Giorgia has a brief but intense love affair with Andrea Berti, a film professor whose off-hand remark ("Quo vadis, baby?") supplies the novel with its title and its clue to the central mystery that Giorgia has been investigating, off and on, for the past twelve years, though not fully aware of it until now. Film buffs may recognize this quotation as a line from Bernardo Bertolucci's famous erotic thriller, *Last Tango in Paris* (1972), starring Marlon Brando as the American ex-patriate Paul and Maria Schneider as the young Parisian Jeanne. Subtly and cogently, Verasani supplies a rich frame of cinematic reference and allusion, which never becomes pretentious or cloying. (Giorgia, in fact, finds that she hates the movie when she forces herself to watch it.) Verasani also suffuses her novel with quotations from favorite bands like Joy Division and The Damned, allusions to writers like Rilke and Schnitzler, and anecdotes (mostly dispiriting) about actors and directors. The artistic and popular culture of Verasani's post-war generation thus serves as a kind of backdrop for the tawdry affairs, humiliations, and betrayals that keep the Cantini agency in business — not to mention the traditional misogyny that continues to pervade twenty-first century Bologna and Italy. Music, in particular, offers Giorgia solace and relief from an increasingly consumerist and impersonal society.

Celebrated for its towers, arcades, and university life, Bologna is an ambivalent figure in the fictional world of Giorgia Cantini. Although not a sentimentalist, Giorgia feels strong nostalgia for the Bologna of her youth — a place where students cared deeply about social justice and political ideals, a place where traditional *osterie* served local dishes, a place that welcomed new art forms, a place enlivened by passionate discussion and debate. As she remarks early on, "Bologna has turned flat, colorless, with no marks of distinction... but nostalgia, I think, has never changed anything." Instead, Giorgia improvises a new kind of community or family with a diverse group of people marginalized from the mainstream values of contemporary Bologna. Although missing a sibling and estranged from her father, she invents new familial and amatory roles for herself and others, roles that both challenge idealized values of the traditional Italian family and openly recognize alternative modes of collective support for the novel's divergent and wayward characters. So Giorgia finds herself acting as a quasi-parent to the forlorn Gaia and as a quasi-older sibling to the know-it-all Tim and as a provisional companion to Lucio, Mel, and other likable loners.

There is a striking contrast between Giorgia's own community and the stream of unhappy clients who come mainly from conventional middle-class and upper-middle-class Bolognese families. In this first novel of the Giorgia Cantini series, Verasani establishes a theme, which will be repeated in each of the four later volumes: the hierarchies and prejudices of "family culture," which many accept as inevitable aspects of everyday life, can lead to tragic acts of violence, demonstrating the vulnerability of those who stray from domestic and sexual norms. In a similar way, the novel makes interesting connections between Giorgia's own family history and the cases that she investigates. Although the detective tries to ignore asking questions about her own past, her professional investigations are never completely separated from reflections about it. Early on in the novel, Verasani suggests the intertwining of Giorgia Cantini's own self-exploration with her professional detective work as she tries to drive home after overindulging at a bar:

> I'm someone who looks forward — to the future. I investigate others, not myself. As for my own black box, I have no desire to find it.
>
> At the first traffic light I open the window and take in the air. I start moving again. I feel drowsy; my mouth tastes bitter; my chest heaves jaggedly. I squint at the rear view mirror; I slip into reverse and back up.

In order to understand both the sexual peccadillos and, at times, the violent cruelty of her clients, Giorgia Cantini cannot avoid examining the practices and values of her own relationships, both past and present. As Alessia Risi comments, "By focusing on the de/construction (of the self) of her protagonist, Verasani reiterates…the importance of proposing a new version of female identity; one that stands out from a background of stereotyped and oppressed female figures, especially in a masculinist genre like crime fiction."[1]

The character of Giorgia Cantini comments acerbically on the facile and idealized notions of Italian-style marriage and kinship, yet imagines new ways of moving forward in an urban space where women can negotiate and create their own "families," which confront historical and cultural inequalities. Giorgia's passionate interest in literature, music, and film also help her construct new strategies for pushing past what she views as the insipid uniformity of contemporary consumer culture. The end of the novel returns to the image of Giorgia in her Citroën literally navigating through her personal and professional life in Bologna, except she is no longer backing up but going forward. While still rubbing the inflamed right eye that has bothered her throughout the narrative, she says in the last line: "I lift my head; I look at A. on the other side of the glass. Then I drive away."

---

1.   Alessia Risi, "Approaches to Gender: Grazia Verasani's Cantini Series." *Out of Deadlock: Female Emancipation in Sara Paretsky's V.I. Warshawski Novels, and Her Influence on Contemporary Crime Fiction*, ed. by Enrico Minardi and Jennifer Byron (Newcastle upon Tyne: Cambridge Scholars Publishing, 2015), 101–115, at 113.

Quo Vadis, Baby?

⊙⊙⊙⊙

Confusion in her eyes that said it all.
She's lost control.
And she's clinging to the nearest passerby.

Joy Division

Quo Vadis, Baby?

I'm sitting on a barstool in Via Goito, clutching the fourth gin bitter of the night. The bartender — a woman in her thirties with striking features and a helmet of flaming red hair — is serving a man in a sleeveless t-shirt with the swelling biceps of a weightlifter. My vision is blurred with booze, and I can't make out the entire place or its occupants. I dimly see reproductions of impressionist paintings on the walls, and a guy with a low brow and hollow eyes smiles vaguely in my direction. I shrug my shoulders and turn my back slowly. I try to stretch my arm muscles, but every movement weighs a ton. My stomach tightens with nausea.

I get off the stool and take two shaky steps; the bartender asks me softly if everything is all right. My heart beats fast, blood rushes to my head, I grab the wooden counter. And she, without emotion: "Maybe you've had too much to drink."

I don't know how I manage to leave the bar. I lean against the door of my old Citroën and light up a Camel.

In a pocket of my windbreaker, there is still a note from Aldo: "Dear Georgia, making the umpteenth move, I've found the letters that Ada sent me from Rome inside a trunk...."

I breathe in the cold winter air and exhale the smoke. I don't know if I'm in any shape to drive. It might be better to walk to the first taxi stand.

I stand still.

It's one in the morning, but I'm too drunk to be aware of time. I almost laugh thinking about all the people who've died after a colossal binge or from mixing booze and pills. Jimi Hendrix, John Belushi....

I step in front of some guy. "Have you ever seen *Splendor in the Grass*?"

He scowls at me, hands deep in the pockets of his orange bomber jacket.

I keep at it: "Come on, that movie with Natalie Wood and Warren Beatty."

He shakes his shaved head and strides confidently into the bar.

I follow and yank him by the sleeve. "She asks him: 'Are you happy?' And Warren answers: 'Don't ask me that question ever again.'"

The guy pushes me aside, and I fall down sobbing, holding my head in my hands. A kind bouncer helps me get up again.

Later, at the wheel, as the artificial lights of the night dazzle my eyes and I try to find my bearings, I'm still lucid enough to feel the weight of that note in my left pocket. I know as soon as I set foot inside my house, if I'm lucky enough to get there, the first thing I'll see on the little glass table in my living room will be a shoe box full of letters written by a person who was alive sixteen years ago.

I turn on the windshield wipers even though it's not raining, and I'm chilled by something I've pushed down, deep inside me. That black well they call "repression," with due respect to psychoanalysis, has always seemed to me the right way to go. No, I don't want to fall into that fucking trap. It doesn't matter that I'm a broken wreck and can't understand why Ada put an end to her life, or why I have this family and not some other one.

I'm someone who looks forward — to the future. I investigate others, not myself. As for my own black box, I have no desire to find it.

At the first traffic light, I open the window and take in the air. I start moving again. I feel drowsy. My mouth tastes bitter. My chest heaves jaggedly. I squint at the rear view mirror. I slip into reverse and back up.

I'm an overweight investigator. I lack the agility you expect from someone in my line of work, but alcohol has strange powers. I thrash inside a laurel hedge and noisily brush my way through.

I find myself in front of Ada's tombstone, next to grandmother Lina's. Just some plastic carnations in a metal vase: even my father hasn't been here for a while.

My mother is somewhere else, in a silver urn, but my sister was buried in a black tube dress with smoky grey stockings. My sister smiles at me from the oval photograph, exactly like my mother at the same age, a bit more than twenty-years old. Grandmother Lina, however, with her aquiline nose, pale subtle lips, and sulky air, seems to say: "It's not so bad here."

I stumble along the gravel path. Inscribed on a tombstone with a little cement angel are the name of a child and just one date: 24 February 1999 — a sign that he was born and died on the same day. I think back on the funeral of my mother: Ada and I dressed the same, her slender body shaken by grief, and mine, stiff and frozen. I left the cemetery watching her dry her tears with the cuff of her green jacket.

I had taken a deep breath. "Let's play a game."

"What kind?" she had asked, fixing me with her hard, red eyes.

And I: "That we're happy, and everything is all right."

Chapter 1

It's cold as hell, but I've turned off the motor to save gas, so I embrace the cold and let it strike the parts of me I've left exposed: face, wrists, ankles. I look in the rear-view mirror: my right eye is bright red. Before going to the agency I should stop at the pharmacy and buy some eye drops. Satie's *Gymnopedie* plays on the car radio as I sit parked in front of a hotel on the outskirts of town, lifeless countryside in the background. This year fall has hurried by and left behind faded, listless colors, self-enclosed like complex-ridden teenagers. I imagine what those two said to each other before hiding away inside here: "Let's leave this world, you and I, for a few hours."

At the hotel window he bends his shoulders and looks outside, breathing in smoke from his cigarette, dark hair and dark eyes, wearing a pale blue shirt with the sleeves rolled up. Behind, on the bed, I get a glimpse of her, hands clasped on her knees and a white bra. With my zoom lens, I see a network of wrinkles around her bright eyes and a worried crease on her cracked lips. Click.

They walk downstairs, pay for the room, and leave the hotel. I follow the Mercedes to the Firefly Restaurant. They go inside. The young waiter welcomes them with a smile. He recognizes them. He helps remove her mink coat; then they sit at a corner table in front of the window. While they glance at the menu, a flower seller moves among the tables. (I hear the sound of back hoes. Somewhere nearby, they're digging the foundation of a new house.) I click again as he takes the cigarette from his mouth and says something like: "You're not feeling well." They look at each other, they laugh. Soon she'll call a taxi and return to her elegant quarters, and he'll go to the office in his Mercedes to finish an important contract. Click. They leave the restaurant and say goodbye with a definite look of intimacy. Click. End of the roll. Also the end of Satie.

The words Cantini Investigative Agency over the doorbell are fading. I enter the double office and open the door to my father's room. He isn't here today.

I sit in his swivel chair and scatter the notes of my last investigation on the walnut desk. The rest of the room features a filing cabinet with ten drawers, a leather arm chair, a bookcase with glass panes, and, in the corner, a sofa with flower-print upholstery.

I open a drawer and find the inevitable bottle of Anisette. Major Fulvio Cantini is no longer a closet drinker. Years ago he was more lucid, more in charge, but now the weight of the agency is almost entirely on my shoulders.

The agency conducts enquiries on behalf of private citizens. We deal with cases of domestic violence, missing persons, and harassment, but above all marital infidelity. On the desk is a computer that my father has never learned to use. He's an old-fashioned man who feels uncomfortable buying mini-cameras or electronic devices for surveillance. He defends field work, the intuition of a true investigator, and he reads too many American crime novels.

The other room has been rented for the past three years to Lucio Spasimo, an IT wizard, who specializes in hardware and software technology. One time he explained to me that his work consists in protecting data from every type of virus and in anti-hacking prevention. Arabic to me.

Spasimo is my age, around forty, strong, near-sighted, and maniacal. I knock at the door of his office. I didn't buy the eye drops: my right eye burns and I feel like rubbing it.

"Hi," says Spasimo without taking his eyes off the PC screen.

I throw myself down on a hard, uncomfortable, and tiny couch. To my right: a floor lamp and a metal chest of drawers. On the walls: a photo of mountain climbers, mountain lakes, and an old calendar of folk artists.

"The lady is fucked," I say.

"Who, the wife of the engineer, Mr. Comolli?

I nod and raise my arms, crossing them behind my head.

"She meets her lover at the Hotel Olympic. Sometimes one day, sometimes another."

"When do you think you'll close the case?"

"Soon." Ritual question: "And you?"

He starts talking about things I don't understand and have no desire to understand. When he finishes, my eyes are half shut and my head sways on the sofa's cement-padded cushion.

"Tim?" I ask.

"Still no sign of him."

Timothy, or Tim, is the enthusiastic young man who acts as my partner with his digital video-camera. He works part-time for the agency and often accompanies me on my stakeouts.

Spasimo points out my olive-green pants. "New?" he asks, as if he didn't know I always wear the same pants and alternate with only one other pair — the same style as these but black and with extra pockets.

I light up a Camel. "All right, I'm going," I say, blowing smoke upward.

Lucio, who hates cigarettes, nods with a sardonic smile and dives again into his PC screen.

The Giordano Lattice file is waiting for me on my desk. Another case solved in a hurry.

Lattice did not show up at the agency like everyone else. He broke a leg on the slopes of Dobbiaco and arranged for me to meet him at his house a few weeks ago.

Four staircases later, I found myself inside the bare apartment of someone half-way moved out: a plant hanging from the ceiling, dirty dishes in the metal sink, boxes of clothes and documents, an oval table, and a pair of plastic chairs.

Lattice, stretched out on a futon in his underwear and blue undershirt, made me notice right away the arching scar above his right eyebrow. "I kept watch outside the house for hours, you know. And when I saw that guy in the BMW open the car door, I lost it. I went blank."

But this happened two years earlier, he told me, when jealousy could still rekindle the passion.

Lying on his side, fully extended, with a spectral voice, he asked me to trail his wife, who had petitioned for a divorce after having kicked him out of the house. Giordano Lattice suspected that she was staying now with a mutual friend of theirs. Reluctant to admit that he still loved her, he claimed to have hired me out of sheer curiosity.

Right now, I have in front of me the photos of Donatella as she leaves a bar, a gym, a tanning salon, a dog pound, a fruit and vegetable shop. Always in the company of a different man. A beautiful woman, Lattice's wife. Long slender body, blonde hair gathered in a braid, haughty green eyes. Forty years lived according to the latest fashion, with distressed jeans and hands thrust inside the pockets of a leather jacket.

I dial Lattice's number, and I imagine him dragging his leg in a cast down the hallway where the telephone sits on the floor amid piles of dust and Marlboro butts. Feeling sure it will lift his spirits to know that his wife spends her time with countless men and not just one, I give him the latest results of my investigation.

After a pause at the other end of the line, I hear a string of "that bitch," "that whore," and so one.

"Calm down, Mr. Lattice…"

"If there's one thing that drives me crazy, it's when someone tells me to calm down!" he yells into the receiver.

And what should I say? "Freak out," "Tear the futon to pieces," "Break your other leg."

"Are you still there?" I ask.

It's unpleasant when people slam the phone in your face before you've had the time to tell them your routing number for a bank deposit.

It's around nine when I park the Citroën in Polese Street. A jazz trio is playing tonight at the Chet Baker Club, and the pianist is a friend of mine.

There are only a few places I go to now. The old trattorias have turned into restaurants that serve bad food and cost an arm and a leg. Aside from Pratello Street, where college students and punk rockers make a racket all night long, ruling the road with their dogs, their joints, their bongs, and their cans of beer, Bologna night life has been flooded by a sea of rich assholes in Range Rovers. And where Range Rovers abound, there can't be much thirst for knowledge.

One day a cabbie told me: "It's not like other cities are different. But here you notice the difference even more, because Bologna used to be a place where a lot happened and where things seemed to work most of the time…"

I go inside the bar and order a gin bitter. As I wait, I feel a hand on my shoulder. "Frank?"

Yes, it's that beast Frank — 225 pounds of sardonic bitterness and eyes so small that, in order to exchange glances, you'd have to stick your fingers between his cheeks and eyebrows to pull them out.

"What are you up to?"

"The Jovanotti tour is over." Frank is a tour manager, always traveling with a band or a famous singer.

"Ah," I say, turning toward the bartender and ordering a gin bitter for Frank. "You want to sit down?" Right then the music stops. The three musicians announce a brief break and leave the stage.

"No, let's talk here."

"And what are we talking about?" If I know Frank, the conversation will be bearable only for someone who has a cocktail of barbiturates waiting on his nightstand.

"You see him"? He points out a balding thirty-something guy sitting at a little table. "He's the one she's seeing now."

"Frank, not to be too nosy…"

"No, no, go ahead," he urges me masochistically.

"Why don't you find yourself a new girl? Maybe there's one on the tour who does catering or works at a booth selling t-shirts…"

I stop midway through my sentence, but in any case Frank is clearly not listening to me. My eyes have just registered on the other side of the bar Alvaro Zincati: straight nose, wavy hair with blonde streaks, and a seductive smirk on his full lips. Alvaro is a lawyer, married with two children. For six months I was his lover, or better yet, his spare wheel.

I gulp down my gin bitter and hear Frank — who has followed the trajectory of my look — say: "I'll defend you from the bad guys."

Alvaro comes by with a glass of white wine in his hand. A nod. "Hi."

"Hi," I answer.

Then he passes on.

A meager "hi" still costs me a pang in the guts. I have a very spiritual intestine. Attempts at reconciliation with the enemy make me feel nauseous.

"You still hate him?" Frank asks.

"No," I smile faintly. "Too much effort."

"But you said hello to him. It's a step forward. I can't do that with Margherita."

I'm tempted to order another gin bitter.

"The real test is to behave as if one has forgiven, though deep down one never forgives," adds Frank, soaked in sweat.

I turn toward him: sweat rings on his t-shirt, a sharp odor, and a satisfied air for this great insight discovered who knows where — certainly not on tour with Lorenzo Cherubini. "A fortune cookie?"

"Seneca," he answers with an Olympian expression.

Out of the corner of my eye, I see Alvaro Zincati leave the club.

Gigi Marini, the pianist, beckons me to join him at his table. I lift my feet from the brass railing that runs along the wooden bar and say goodbye to Frank.

Two in the morning. Time to slip on a condom, rock the room a little, and once again we're two old pals who drink and smoke in the dark.

Gigi has a transparent expression and sloping shoulders — nothing to do with being a Walkman-toting cyclist. But he has a dazzling smile that rejuvenates him, despite the gap between his incisors and the perennial dark circles under his eyes. "Do you ever see Vasari?" he asks.

"I know he's set up a news stand."

"He was tired of the late nights."

"He must be making more money."

Gigi thinks about it a bit, and then turns toward me: "Why don't you start playing again?"

At twenty, I played drums in a group. I couldn't keep time, and the public terrified me. They had to make me drink two straight vodkas, fasten the sticks in my hands, and shove me onto the stage. As soon as I met someone's glance, I lost the beat, dismantled the framework of the songs, or went into a wild frenzy of rhythmic abandon.

I look at him. "You've got to be joking?"

My tongue is dry, his bladder is full. He makes a kind of smirk and goes off to the bathroom. After a few minutes, I hear him arrange the sheets, snorting, and then we go to sleep.

The morning after, I stumble bare-foot down the hallway, rubbing my sleep-crusted eyes. When I glimpse the shadow of someone in my kitchen, my first impulse is to yell "stop!" and pull out my gun, if I had one. Then I remember: there is a jazz piano player in my house who, considerately, is making me breakfast.

"No point in searching; I don't have any sweets or biscotti."

"Good morning," he says in the hoarse voice of someone who has smoked to the end of one day and begun the next in the same way. "You've got a red eye."

"Yep," I answer, ripping the paper out of his hand so I can take the first look.

We sit on stools facing each other. As we drink our coffee, he tells me that he's already read the horoscope for Cancer (we both have the same crappy astrological sign). "It appears that next year will be fantastic: money, love, work…"

"Let's hope so. Last year was shit."

"The horoscopes never get us right," he says pulling on a green sweater with elbow patches.

"Exactly."

It takes a quarter of an hour for me to get down from my stool. I reach the bathroom walking unsteadily on the parquet floor. I turn on the shower just in time to hear Gigi Marini, getting dressed in the bedroom, say: "I'm playing tonight at Chet Baker."

"Maybe I'll drop by," I yell through the door.

"Great."

We both know I won't drop by.

When the front door closes, I leave the bathroom and make my way through stockings and tops scattered on the floor, piles of CDs, overflowing ashtrays, newspapers, and dirty cups. A cold, late January sun beats against the window panes spotted by a recent rain. I close the shutters, get dressed, zip up my wind breaker, and tuck my short hair under a wool beret. I hear the bells of Saint Joseph the Laborer and the noise of light Sunday traffic. I climb into the Citroën and drive to the second-hand record market, a warehouse in the area of North Park converted for the buying and selling of every musical fetish.

Davide Melloni, Mel to his friends, is at his stall — boxes overflowing with vinyl records. He has a three-day-old salt and pepper beard and a noteworthy nose like the actor Toto. He played the bass in my group, ages ago, and now and then we say hello to each other. What unites us, aside from old times, is an undying love for Punk. Mel and I loved The Damned. I still remember how pissed off he'd get if someone reduced Punk to a music genre. "Punk is an attitude!" he'd scream.

He used to go to London to buy up old records, which he'd then resell at full price to Bologna Punk fans camped out in front of The Golden Record. Today he has one of the most popular catalogs among wealthy Japanese clients. He buys stuff at auction on the internet, and he runs a website with a mailing list of fanatical followers, who spend exorbitant sums for a vinyl album of The Stranglers or The Sex Pistols. And then he travels the world: London, Manchester, Paris, Barcelona, often in the company of Tito, a gay trade-show exhibitor who specializes in Italian music.

I see him from afar haggling over the price of a record with a boy in hip-hop attire. I approach his stall.

"A DJ," he says, glancing at the guy who just left with a basketful of vinyl. "Lounge and chill-out music is back in fashion. These guys buy everything."

We're not friends who hug each other. "How about a coffee?" I propose.

He gestures to Tito to keep an eye on the merchandise, takes me by the arm, and we walk the short distance that separates us from the bar.

"I haven't bought music in a while," I tell him.

"Music today is the same as back then."

"What do you mean?"

"It's either good or bad."

He orders a coffee for me and a Montenegro with ice for himself.

"Having a good day?"

He shrugs his shoulders, rubbing his hands on his knees. "I've sold all the vinyl Ramones, and I confess I'm a little heart-broken."

I nod, nostalgic. He sips his Montenegro and wets his lips. "You still listen to The Who?" He still hasn't forgotten my love for that drummer who used to play so softly that the cymbals seemed to whisper.

I mix some diet sweetener in my coffee and smile thinly. "Every now and then."

"Always alone?"

I raise my eyes from the cup. "Always alone."

"You weren't a bad drummer, you know."

I punch him affectionately.

"Before…" He doesn't finish the phrase. "Everything changed after what happened."

"What happened" refers to my sister Ada.

"Yes, everything changed," I say looking at the ground.

"Sorry, I didn't mean to bring it up. It's just that when I see you…"

"It's normal. Don't worry."

"Back to work," he says. I go with him part of the way toward his stall. "See you later, Mel."

Next day I wake up early and go to the agency. In front of the door, on the faded mat, is a brown package. I pick it up.

The sender is Aldo Cinelli, an old friend of my sister who's been living in London for several years where he works, I believe, as a writer. I'm puzzled.

I enter the office, put the package on the desk, open it, and find a shoe box jam-packed with envelopes. I immediately recognize the handwriting. Aldo has added a handwritten note: "Dear Giorgia, after the umpteenth move, I've found the letters that Ada used to send me from Rome inside a trunk. I think it's better for you to keep them. Hugs, Aldo."

My heart stops briefly. I rush into Spasimo's office, sure that I'll find him. I suspect that he sleeps here some nights, fully dressed, on top of the sofa that's as comfortable as cement.

He focuses on the box I'm holding in my hand. "So you've bought yourself a pair of Reeboks?"

I shut my eyes halfway. "She never once wrote to me," I say in a low voice.

Spasimo sighs, his chest heaving. He sits astride the chair and rubs his arms (hairy even down to the backs of his hands). This is what he knows about Ada: she was my only sister, two years older. She wanted to be an actress, and she lived in Rome. One morning, Giulio, her boyfriend, returning from a weekend with his family, opened the door to the apartment on Piazza Malva and found her hanging from a beam in the ceiling.

The autopsy revealed a high level of alcohol in the blood, and the police determined that her suicide was the extreme reaction of an aspiring out-of-work actress. A neighbor saw a man, who was never identified, leave the apartment at dawn.

Things that happened sixteen years ago. Things that no one here in the agency ever talks about, out of respect to the Major and me — the subject is always off limits. Things that everyone knows about.

I show Spasimo the note from Aldo.

"Do you intend to read them?" he asks, nodding at the contents of the box.

"I don't know."

I see his large and subtle mouth open to say something and then stop. At that moment the doorbell rings.

The woman sitting in front of me on the leather armchair calls herself Lucia Tolomelli. She's about thirty-five years old. A flowery scarf bought at some open-air market wraps her small, oblong head. She's slender all the way to her waist, but down below she sprouts a housewife's ass and shapely legs crammed into a pair of tan gabardine pants.

I'm still stunned by the surprise package. It takes me a while to regain my professional composure. I set aside the box and take up a pen and paper.

Lucia Tolomelli is here to talk to me about her husband Alfio, who is perhaps having an affair with her cousin Maria Veronesi.

There's a crease in her broad brow. Behind layers of dark foundation, I glimpse tiredness and sleepless nights. She has black hair, dull and limp, that she fingers continuously, and damp eyes that make me suspect she's just been crying. I ask her if she'd like a glass of water. She shakes her head politely and starts to talk.

"For me Maria is like a sister. The other day, I brought her home-made tagliatelle, and I could tell from her expression that something was bothering her. My husband always found her attractive, and I've always felt there was some bond between them…" She pauses. "After work he usually goes to the Ulysses Bar to play cards, but there are many evenings that I call there and don't find him. Then I call Maria and don't find her either. In short, perhaps I'm making everything up, but if you were to find some evidence…"

There it is. Evidence. Is Lucia Tolomelli a fan of *Colombo*? Or maybe she watches *Cops*? *LA Law*?

While she recounts the creative lies of her husband, I feel like I'm at the movies watching a crime drama with a predictable plot. Scene One: the policeman approaches the body. Scene Two: the policeman vomits off to the side. In certain cases you can anticipate everything beforehand.

Despite her embarrassment and timidity, Lucia has the excited voice and television ego of someone who has voluntarily taken on a fictional role.

Staying true to my role, I pose the questions she's used to hearing on TV, even if, to ease my bad conscience, I imagine charitably the home where she lives: the curtains she has lovingly embroidered, the endless wait to put her kids to bed, the ear straining to hear the sound of an engine, the clicking of the cuckoo clock on the mantle. The Furies rising up to scream vengeance. The jealousy that attacks the mind of a woman who has a subscription to *People Magazine* and puts her hair in curlers all alone. The anxiety. The extra pounds she curses in front of the mirror, thinking about how much younger and prettier her cousin Maria is.

I take notes: Alfio works at Esselunga in Casalecchio di Reno. I write down their home address and that of Maria, a clerk in a shoe store on Bentini Street.

Lucia takes from her brown leather purse a couple of photos. "I never thought I'd do something like this," she murmurs, rising from the armchair and putting on her synthetic burgundy jacket.

"Don't worry," I reassure her.

She smiles weakly and gives me a hard look. "Do you have conjunctivitis?"

Automatically I touch my right eye with my hand.

"You should see an optometrist," she advises me.

I thank her. I say I'll call her soon, and ask her to kindly close the door when she leaves.

As soon as I'm alone, I drag the shoebox to the center of the desk.

We've been here for over an hour, in front of the Olympic Hotel, in my icy car with the quirky battery.

Tim is tall and gangly. He has blonde unruly hair on a pale white brow, chestnut eyes and high cheekbones. Under his jacket he wears a t-shirt with the motto *LEGALIZE CANNABIS*.

"I was up late last night at the disco," he yawns.

"Discos still exist?"

He straightens his skinny back against the seat and gives me a puzzled look. "What sort of question is that?"

"Do you like them?"

"Yeah, the amplification…the basses that pierce your ear drums…"

"Fine. Can you still hear?"

He looks up at the car roof, smoking. "There's no point talking to you. You're too bitter."

Like it or not, I'm also inhaling marijuana.

"I'd like to get a band together," he says, puffing a cloud of smoke.

"But didn't you want to shoot a short feature?"

"Yeah, that too. Ah, the digital revolution!" he gets excited. "At one time, you worked only with film, but now anyone can make his own movie, you know. It's the same with music. You buy a computer, and you create, compose, make records at home. Even if you don't know how to play. This is real democracy!"

"Perhaps …"

"Oh, you're just like the others," he groans.

"How so?" I'm not eager to know.

"They hang weights around our necks, and they drag us down."

I glance at the shoebox on the back seat. "Come on, pass me that joint."

In the bedroom on the first floor, the curtains are drawn. Who knows how long we'll have to wait before something happens? I turn toward Tim; he aims my Nikon at me. Mrs. Comolli and her lover leave the hotel at that moment, I tug at Tim to change direction, and he, in a flash, immortalizes a secret kiss.

"Those two love each other, and we're here to screw up their lives."

I mutter my skepticism and light up a Camel. "You're too good, Tim."

"If I had a girl, I wouldn't cheat on her."

I burst out laughing.

He looks at me with disgust. "You don't believe me?"

"Yes, yes, I believe you…"

"I don't want to end up like you, boss."

"Thanks."

A quarter of an hour later I drop Tim off at his scooter.

I pass the evening drinking at the bar on Via Goito.

I break the law going secretly into the Certosa cemetery.

And now here I am: three in the morning, after a cold shower and three cups of coffee, half-naked on my green velvet living room sofa.

I draw Ada's letters from the box and start reading haphazardly.

"Georgia would never understand my affair with A., she doesn't know what it means, she isn't the type and never will be. You know her, boys don't interest her…"

Further on: "When he goes away, I feel dizzy. With A., I'm everything I can't be with Giulio. I don't want my sister to know these things…"

Another letter: "We've seen *Last Tango in Paris* for the third time. I adore that film. Perhaps it's too strong, and A., sometimes he scares me. What do I know about him? Nothing…"

I'm unable to think. It's like reading the life of a stranger.

I bring my nose close to the paper to sense if there is still some smell of her. A drop of coffee falls on the date of the page. I repeat mentally the last phrase, and meanwhile I try to soak up the stain. "A., sometimes he scares me."

Who was this A.? He appears in other letters, but always and only with the initial, never with the full name. Did Giulio know of his existence?

Memories of the university swarm in my head like flies around a lamplight. At the time I was enrolled in law school. I had watched Ada drag two huge suitcases behind her and board a train straight for the capital. Giulio had begun to work for *Il Messaggero* and waited for her in a tiny rented apartment.

It was an indisputable fact for me that Ada had talent. I did not see her doing anything besides reading comedies, going to the theatre, studying speech and diction, learning monologues by heart to present at auditions… Her favorite passage was from *Fraulein Elsa* by Schnitzler, and she rehearsed it in front of the large mirror of our bedroom.

We didn't look like each other, my sister and I. If you saw us, you wouldn't think we came from the same person. Ada was slender and wiry like an electric cord, plus she was blonde and forever smiling, but above all she was the only true artist of the house. My father and I never talked about her death, each of us closed up in our own defensive silence. Right away, I went to live by myself, and he poured himself into opening the agency.

Four in the morning. I drink a little more coffee and throw myself on the sofa.

I'm not sleepy, but I close my eyes and see my father, once again, fill a small travel bag and leave for Rome in a big hurry.

For a few months, I investigate the mysterious man seen by an old neighbor leaving Ada's apartment at dawn. Giulio knew nothing about it and refused to accept the idea that Ada was seeing somebody else. Their mutual friends were interrogated by the police. Not one of them was with her that night. For them, Ada and Giulio made a tight couple.

Ages ago, I stopped asking why my sister killed herself. At the time, it didn't seem disturbing that she would have a lover. She was young, beautiful, and full of life. She could have had the conventional love affair, or perhaps it was just some guy she barely knew whom she brought home that night, taking advantage of Giulio's absence. I put the letters aside. Then I look at them again.

A. as in Alberto, Antonio, Andrea, Alex, Alfredo… Who is A.? What part did he have in all of this?

For Doctor Ciacioni there were no doubts.

"Suicide," he said to my father, with the honesty one reserves for someone in the profession. The autopsy spoke loud and clear. No other explanation. Case closed. Like Ada in her coffin.

I hide the box in a drawer under a pile of clothes. An infantile gesture, to avoid seeing those letters on the table again when I wake up.

Why should I have to read words that serve no purpose anymore?

As usual, Aldo has acted thoughtlessly, or perhaps he was truly convinced that he was doing me a favor.

I ask myself if he, my sister's confidant, knows who A. is.

I ask myself if A. was with her when she did what she did.

CHAPTER 2

I live at the intersection between the highway that goes to the sea and the one that goes to Milan. When I leave the house, all I see, apart from the headquarters of the Democrats of the Left where they serve plates of polenta and sausage every Sunday, are Chinese. They don't know how to drive — the Chinese — but this is an irrelevant detail.

A few nights ago, a police flyer was put up on Carlo Porta Street. Apparently, some Chinese were using the basement of an apartment building as a warehouse or a workshop, with loud machinery operating right through the night, so people called 911.

In front of the mail slot, I run into my second-floor neighbor, a pleasant widow. We often chat about the weather or seasonal ailments.

"Don't you think we're living in Chinatown?"

She looks at me confused, but just like me she woke up one day to find no more grocery stores, dry cleaners, or local shops. In their place: shops for Chinese handbags, Chinese delis, and Chinese clothes. Before the Chinese came, there were only old-fashioned restaurants with fish tanks; now they arrive, they pay in cash, and you can't go three feet without seeing almond-eyed people selling you goods made in China. At Covered Cross Park, in front of the Casa Buia Restaurant (where long ago the naval canal carried travelers to Venice and where now a devoted group of retirees looks after the ducks and Australian swans), there's not yet sign of Chinese doing Tai Chi. But it's only a matter of time.

My neighbor says she's afraid of the Mafia. For her the Chinese, Albanian, or Russian Mafia is the same thing. You lose trust when they take away the business right in front of you that used to sell you fresh bread and stracchino. This is what pisses me and my neighbor off.

I say goodbye, leave the building, and walk to my car. Yet Chinese or no Chinese, I'm content to be in this neighborhood, far from the city center turmoil, the bureaucrats, the night clubbers.

I drive past the former Red Barracks, still haunted by the ghosts of many partisan members. Up until fifteen years ago, there was a recording studio where local bands created their own demos. A bright poster on the door bore the signature of Andrea Pazienza.

Bologna has turned really flat, colorless, with no marks of distinction...but nostalgia, I think, has never changed anything.

I park the Citroën outside the agency. I have an appointment in ten minutes, just in time to have breakfast at the bar. After a coffee and pastry, I ask Enzo, the bartender, if I can use the telephone.

Aldo answers after five rings.

"What's the weather like there?" I ask.

"Typical," he says in a nasal voice. "It's been raining non-stop for a week, and it's cold as hell."

Even though he's lived in London for ten years, he hasn't lost his pronounced Bologna accent.

"I wanted to thank you for the letters..."

I hear him yawn. "You know, I didn't recall even having them anymore."

Pause.

"Listen...but this A., who is he?"

Silence at the other end of the line. After a few moments: "I have no idea."

"Aldo, those letters were addressed to you."

"We were friends, Alda and I."

I stiffen up hearing him say my sister's name. She seems real, and she's not anymore.

"The only thing I know is that he wanted to be an actor and studied for a while at the university."

"That's all?"

"Yes, that's all. Well, no. Ada told me that he wasn't from Rome but from Emilia-Romagna like us…from Parma perhaps or from Reggio Emilia, I don't remember…"

"She never dropped his name?"

"She said he had to remain an entity."

"An entity?"

He sighs. "Yes, an entity."

"Take care, Aldo."

"You, too."

When I enter the agency, Spasimo lets me know there's a new client waiting in my office.

As soon as I open the door, a fat young man with tawny hair exclaims, "Good morning!" He shakes my hand and introduces himself: "Alvise Lumini, it's a pleasure to meet you."

He looks like a Sunday school teacher — toothy and awkward.

"Take a seat," I motion to the arm chair.

He sits down and coughs to clear his voice. "I'll explain quickly. I'm from Belluno. I've lived here a few years…I've opened a small office. I'm an orthodontist." He looks at me, quite pleased with himself.

(What does he want, applause?)

"Go on," I urge him.

"The name of my fiancée is Serena Battaglia. She's twenty-nine and lives at 43 Gombruti Street."

I look at him, waiting.

"Well," he stammers, "I've had some last-minute doubts, let's say."

(As if I don't get it.)

"All right…I'm a jealous type. I need some kind of guarantee."

"Such as knowing what Serena is up to when you aren't together and who she dated before you."

"Exactly."

"Why don't you ask Serena these things yourself?"

He looks down. "If I could do that, I wouldn't be asking for your help."

"Fair enough," I admit.

"I have a mother with a bad heart, plus five brothers. They'll all be coming down from Belluno for the wedding…"

I motion for him to keep going.

"I'd like Serena to make a good impression on my family. I wouldn't want to discover…some stains, you understand?"

"Do you have suspicions?"

"Absolutely not. She's a fine girl, she works in a dress shop, she's a wizard with the sewing machine, but…"

(There's always a "but.")

"Every time we go to the restaurant there's at least one man that says hello to her."

"Maybe she has lots of friends."

"Yes, but I'd like to know more about it. You know, you only get married once in your life…"

I burst out laughing. "My god, sometimes people get married even seven times."

"That's not the case with me," he hisses.

I press my lips. "Sure, sure."

I hand him a routine information form, I make him put down a deposit, and I dismiss him. "I'll keep you informed."

Alvise Lumini gets up from the chair and gives me a vigorous handshake.

After eating a sandwich at the bar, and despite the umpteenth coffee, I find myself leaning my head on my office desk. I'm worn out.

What happened to Ada's things? Most likely the same as Mama's things. It was Aunt Lydia, my father's sister, who packed up everything: part for the poor, part for herself. I managed to save a pink sweater for myself and a pearl necklace, which ought to be in some corner of the storage room. I only have a few photos of Ada and an engagement ring, a gift from Giulio, which I keep in a small drawer with my other jewelry. She must have had an appointment book, I tell myself, with the numbers of her friends in Rome and the people she confided in. I could contact them. To know what? What's there for me to know? My father returned from Rome empty-handed and behaved exactly as he did when my mother died. Make everything disappear, keep nothing: that's his solution. He has always made decisions for me.

"My name is Livio... Antonio... Marescalchi."

The guy I have in front of me — neck buried in his shoulders and black hair flaking dandruff on a sleek electric blue shirt — has taken two entire minutes to tell me his name, with oratorical pauses.

He acts like the owner of a shady business, but he's just told me he works on the internet. I haven't dared to ask anything else. I've slept three hours, I'm a wreck, and this irritating man has shown up without any advance notice.

"Listen, not to make you hurry..."

He stares at me with glassy eyes, lashes lowered. I ask myself what sort of sedative he uses. Seroxat, Elopram, or something stronger.

"It began three months ago," he tells me, speeding up his tempo slightly. "I chat online."

"So do lots of people."

He glances at me, and I gather that I should not interrupt him: if he loses the thread of his discourse, we might be here all night.

"At the beginning, with Tiziana, we wrote each other lines from movies we liked the most, and also phrases from songs. She's fond of light music. I'm not so keen on...pop."

I bite the end of my pen, waiting, stretching my legs under the desk.

"Then we moved on to personal stuff, like where you live, how old you are, what's your job, what do you think about love...Tiziana is thirty-one, I'm thirty-five."

I restrain myself from astonishment: I would have said forty at the very least.

"She lives at San Giovanni in Persiceto."

"That's not far."

"True."

Silence.

"Would you care for something to drink?" I sigh.

"I…I'm not afraid of death."

Perhaps I have a killer in front of me who will soon confess to having chopped up Tiziana's body and hidden it in the garage.

"But of love…yes. Love is a lot fiercer," he maintains in a solemn tone.

I nod, asking myself if now's the time to call Spasimo on any pretext whatsoever.

Marescalchi takes my pack of Camels and my Bic and lights himself a cigarette without asking permission. I let him.

"We've declared our love."

"Without ever seeing each other?"

"Yes."

"Not even in a photograph?"

"Yes."

"I don't want to question your judgment, but in these cases…the online chats, the emails, these virtual things, except in the rarest situations…"

"We saw each other last Monday in Piazza San Francisco," he says crushing the cigarette in half in the ashtray. "And she got upset there."

"That is?"

"She told me it was a mistake for us to meet, and then she confessed that she was married." He leans towards me, elbows planted on the desk. "My question is: does she really have a husband?"

I cough. "And so you're here because you want to know if Tiziana is really married?"

"What do you think?"

"About what, excuse me?"

"About all this business. I'd like to have your opinion."

"Listen, I'm an investigator, not a psychologist."

"Tiziana had never told me…"

"Pardon me, but how does this change anything? Married or unmarried, Tiziana doesn't want to see you again, right? Or has she continued writing you?"

"No, she's stopped writing."

"Let's put it this way, Marescalchi, perhaps you haven't struck a spark."

His eyes grow wide. "Do I seem so ugly to you?"

"No, I didn't say that…" I bend my head to the side, careful to measure my words. "Let's say that maybe she was frightened. Not of your appearance. She simply hadn't considered the reality of it all."

(Here I go, playing the psychologist.)

"In…in what sense?"

"Well, sometimes the idea you've created about someone is more important than the person himself. Do you understand?"

"I don't think so."

I stare at him for a moment. "Tiziana doesn't like you, pure and simple."

He nods, showing self-control, then rises softly from the chair. "You don't want to help me out, do you?"

"I'm certainly helping you out. I won't ask a penny for the half hour you've made me waste. And since I consider myself a generous person, I'll give you some advice. Stop the online chatting and go to a bar, or Club Med, or, if you prefer, to a private club."

Afterwards, I show him the door.

My trade has its pros and cons. When he opened the agency, my father told me: "It should remain an artisan's job." This was his way of telling me that we weren't one of those big firms that base their investigations on advances in technology. The problem is that today technological tools are fundamental.

Just think of all the cases solved because of intercepted telephone conversations, searching data bases, phone logs, connections between one call and another…

We don't concern ourselves with industrial crimes or investigations. I've never taken a course for detectives, but I understood immediately that in this line of work when you find yourself in the middle of the street wondering whether to go right or left, you've got to rely on your instinct. Either you have a nose for the job or you don't.

From the client's point of view, the good thing about a small agency is that you make a deposit, with the understanding that "we'll work it out." We say this to clients who aren't dripping in gold. The fact that I'm a woman has never surprised anyone. Everyone has seen *Charlie's Angels*, and people are amazed that I don't carry a gun, even though I sometimes have to note that a woman, during a stakeout, draws less attention than two men in a car or one man reading a newspaper next to a lamp post.

At the end of an investigation, I write a report, sign it, and give it to my client. It's the only desk work I do. Everything else is the street.

My cases mainly involve cheating spouses or cuckolds wearing the proverbial horns. The majority of my clients are women, and ninety-nine per cent already know they have them — the horns — but they need to hear it clearly and unequivocally. Then there are those who deny the evidence that lawyers put in front of them and those who doubt the crushing truth of their own eyes. Almost no one comes here in an effort to save their marriage: they all scream for vengeance.

But I sometimes have to follow anorexic or bulimic daughters, drug-addicted children, alcoholic husbands, chronic gamblers, lost cats. The client wanted to know: is she eating or not? Is she vomiting in the bathroom or not? Is he doping himself or not? Drinking or not? Gambling or not? And so I trailed the addict or the pusher in dodgy places, plunked down small bets in some casino, hid behind the bathroom door of a bar to hear suspicious noises. Or I found myself astride a tree limb, my hands scratched up like a pissed-off monkey.

A stakeout is never the way you see it in the movies. You often have to check the place out the day before. Every spot has its trapdoors, its peculiar features, and you have to memorize the details. When you go on foot, you have to learn to keep a certain distance. It takes only a second to lose someone in a crowd, or to reveal yourself. If the man or woman stops in front of a shop window or suddenly decides to change streets, you have to be able to see their moves beforehand. In short, you can't be distracted or waste time deliberating.

In some situations, the adrenaline will be pumping, but there's nothing romantic about investigating. At least not for me. If a client is satisfied because you've resolved a case, then that's a good thing, but it's no fun having to explain to someone that the person they love is seeing another lover every Thursday.

"A detective doesn't judge," my father told me several years ago when he opened the agency. You don't always succeed. When some guy doesn't want to support his family, or spend time with his kids, and yet maintains that he's a saint despite the photos of him wrapped around his wife's best friend…it's a real ball-buster.

I've done this work for fourteen years, and some cases I'll never forget. There was Gigliola, the prostitute, in love with a bus driver, who came to me because she wanted to know his schedule and take the bus when he was driving. Mrs. Pia Galimberti, who suspected her husband, a company executive, of cheating and collapsed when she learned that her beloved spouse was having sex with transvestites. Then Eugenia Lippi, whose husband had squandered one business and three apartments at the roulette wheel. And finally Professor Carlini, who feared the effects of cosmic rays on his apartment and ended up enclosing his windows in lead…

One thing is certain: when the agency began, I had more enthusiasm, perhaps because I didn't yet know that I'd be caught up in domestic dramas, sick love stories, triangles.

I've always kept a small book with a yellow cover that I dug up at a book stall and that still sits in plain view on a shelf in my office. It's called *The Young Detective's Manual*, and it was written in 1971 by Mario Nardone, a police commissioner and later assistant prosecutor, famous for arresting the Monday Gang, a band of bank robbers who operated, only on Mondays, from 1961 to 1965.

I've underlined page after page, discovering so many little marvels. Now the cover is creased and full of loose pages, but when I first had it, I passed entire nights in its company.

I annotated the essential qualities of a detective. I discovered the comparison microscope, microfilm, computers, and then radio microphones, re-transmitters, mini-cameras in the shape of cigarette cases. I understood police records, how a handwriting analysis works, what a forensic doctor and a ballistic expert do.

It fascinated me that all human beings have fingerprints that stay the same from birth to death, that tests can determine the maximum life span of a human hair to be four years, that women have about 240,000 feet of hair and that a beard is made up of around fifteen thousand hairs. I looked at the designs of Peruvian *quipos* and their messages encoded in a sequence of knots, the photos of Parisian thugs known as Apaches, dancing the Java, with their tattoos, their *gigolettes*, and their knife fights. I read about card sharks and marked poker decks, about candles used as anti-theft devices by Leonardo Da Vinci to safeguard the Sforza treasures, about famous escapes, distinguished swindlers, and charming counterfeiters.

I learned the jargon of criminals: for example, that a gun in Bari is a "jerk off," a "Bertha" in Rome, and a "rabid woman" in Milan; that a "countess" is a strong box, that a "butterfly" is a letter, that "to slog" means to steal money, and that "to cop a smoke" means to steal tobacco; that "it's a foggy night" means to put off the job for another day; that "go into second gear" in Venice means to "bolt it"; and that in Palermo you keep your mouth shut with "closed teeth."

Thanks to Nardone, I discovered that Al Capone was the son of a hair dresser from Naples, that Pinkerton, the best-known detective agency in the world, was founded in Chicago in 1850, and that the setting of the Simenon/Maigret novels was the police department of Quai des Orfevres 36...

That book, however dated, gave me a lot of inspiration, even if the Cantini Agency was imposed on me by my father as repayment for being a college dropout.

I get home at eight in the evening, tired and hungry. I go to the kitchen and take an out-of-date carton of beans from the fridge. I heat up the mush and eat it standing up, one spoonful after another. Then, thinking of nothing, I go to my bedroom, pull the shoe box from the closet, light a Camel, and begin to read...

February 12, 1985

Dear Aldo,

I like Trastevere. I adore these little streets with their restaurants, shops, and flowered terraces. Now and then I come across someone famous, especially when I go to the market at the Campo de' Fiori. I spend the day at bars smearing coffee cups with lipstick and writing down important phone numbers in my address book, numbers for work. Some mornings I make the casting rounds with my portfolio, carry back my head shot in my purse, throw it on the desk, and plant it there like you would on a roulette wheel...

May 3, 1985

Movie City. Theatre 5. They're looking for extras on a film by Celantano. Before leaving the house, I do an imitation of Joan Collins and say to Giulio: "I'm going and coming back with dollars!" I arrive at the audition completely soaked (today it rained a lot), with bits of tomato from a slice of pizza in the corners of my mouth. I take a seat on stage, hide my face in my hands, and think of my mother...

June 11, 1985

God, how much I detest actors and their phony voices. If you saw me now, Aldo... Remember when we used to play bocce at the beach in Savio, and I always won? Well, now I feel disgustingly weak, and I'm having panic attacks. Two nights ago, Giulio called the doctor, and he gave me an injection. Every time I go inside the bathroom, G. is scared that I'll do something foolish...

September 12, 1985

I met A. at an audition. We've been seeing each other for a week and, so far, Giulio isn't suspicious. This affair won't turn into something serious, I know. We're in a rush to consume each other and leave without paying. I've read your story, "The Pine Grove of the Angels." Really beautiful.

October 3, 1985

Audition at Theatre Argentina. More than two hundred hopefuls for the role. I would have liked to yell: "We're all in deep shit, girls!" but we preferred to be catty with each other and inflate our resumés. There was one girl who told me the audition was over and then there she was, in line, right behind me. What a bitch... You ask me about A., but I can't talk about him. I beg you not to say a word about this to Giorgia. She's fond of Giulio and thinks I'm living it up here, with only one passion: the theatre. If only she knew how much I'm starting to hate it, the theatre! Last Tango in Paris *is A.'s favorite film. Now I know all the lines by heart...*

November 10, 1985

Audition at the Scaparro. Three hundred people, two hundred and thirty of them women, and the cast for It was Mattia Pascal *already wrapped up. What a joke, what a ruse just to get government subsidies!*

I leave A.'s house and take a walk, I look at the rat-infested Tiber, and go up and down the Ponte Sisto at sunset with the Gianicolo Hill in front of me. Then I enter the Church of Santa Maria della Scala and pray for my artistic career. Oh, oh, oh. For a single line of a script, I'd dance naked in Via Condotti...

November 23, 1985

I bought a pregnancy test at the pharmacy. You'd have to be completely senseless to bring someone into this world. A. is seeing other women, I'm sure of it. We fuck, we drink, we snort cocaine…

My eyes are puffy with sleep. I open a bottle of Four Roses and a new pack of Camels.

It's raining today. The Tiber at full tide covers the Tiber Island. Big cities scare me. There's so much of this city, too much. I look at the drama library that lies on my book shelves. It would only take a match to burn up all the pages I've never acted out. I have an ideal theatre, inside me, and I defend it. Even here, you know, as everywhere else, they treat me like somebody strange.

December 4, 1985

Breakfast at the Malva Bar reading the paper: I want to die. You write that my sister is furious because I don't write to her. The problem is that I'd have to write lies to her and I can't do it. Keep an eye on her, even if she doesn't need it, and send me other stories to read. Who knows, one day you'll be writing for me…

Yesterday evening, an aperitif at the Hemingway (Rupert Everett was there), then the Bar della pace, Le Corracchie, and finally dinner at Le Fontane. I told Giulio that I was sleeping over at a girlfriend's place and instead spent the night with A. listening to The Lounge Lizards in the dark.

When they ask me who my favorite actress is, I always answer Piera Degli Esposti in Molly, My Dear, *but you're right, Glenda Jackson in* The Servants *isn't too bad. Heartfelt thanks for the money order. I received it yesterday. I don't have a penny and I've hocked two rings and a bracelet, even the gold chain that Giorgia gave me.*

Incredible, it snows here too… It's awful going back to G.'s house after having made love with A. I think that my love for G. is like a kitchen apron, while my love for A. is an evening dress with a low neckline. He gets rough when he drinks… I think I'm not going to call home for a while. The other day my father told me that with my personality I'll never have a career.

I get up and run down the hallway to the bathroom. On my knees, with my head in the toilet, I vomit the bean puree.

CHAPTER 3

I've transcribed a few sentences from the letters onto a note pad, and I read them now at traffic lights. The last year of my sister's life is all there in those scattered pages.

I have the sensation of watching the world through a window. I try to kick and smash to get through it, but it's thick and unbreakable. It's been years since I felt like this.

I ought to work, finish the investigations underway, earn my daily bread, and instead there are other things going on in my head. I drive the streets at a normal pace, and certain phrases of Ada roll in my mind like marbles. *When he drinks, he gets rough…*

Later, sitting at my office desk, I light up a cigarette and look at my notes. Alfio Tolomelli, Alvise Lumini. Distractedly, with a red pen, I draw a circle around the first initial of the two names.

When the door bursts open, the black and white pictures of old Bologna jolt on the walls. My father has a heavy step. (Cantini, my mother called him. I don't remember her ever calling him by his first name.)

"What's wrong with your eye?" he asks.

"I don't know, maybe a gnat got inside it."

He opens the paper that he's holding under his arm. "The Conservatives have won even in Holland."

"And aren't you glad, Papa?" I say, still looking at my notes.

He glances at the turned-on computer. "Is that box really necessary?"

"You don't live in the modern world."

Awkward and embarrassed as always, in the presence of my father, Lucio enters and greets him. Fulvio Cantini puts a hand on his shoulder and spreads the newspaper.

"Dear Spasimo, the Left went out with the Seventies, when they murdered Moro. You need to say that to all the guys dancing round in circles."

Spasimo nods submissively.

I bite the tip of my pen between my teeth. My father still has the power to make me nervous like a school girl who hasn't done her homework.

"All those guys with their portable gadgets…" he goes on, "I see them in the cafes, making investments, following the ups and downs of the market, scanning the business pages. A generation of marketing experts. But do they ever get it right?"

I'm distracted. *I eat four oranges a day to pay for a discount theatre ticket, and a director says he'll give me the part of Ophelia if I'm sweet to him…*

The Major takes off his overcoat. He's wearing a light champagne sweater. I'm afraid he intends to stay longer than usual, and I go blank gazing at the clothing store sign that I glimpse through the window. Now he leans on the bookshelf like someone who resigned many years ago, not just from the carabinieri. I look at him. He's no longer the same man who dutifully looked after two girls orphaned by their mother. Life has turned him into a sad drunk with a vacant and sullen expression.

I remember the time, a little after Ada's death, when the doctor came to the house and told him he ought to go easy on the booze. My father answered that drinking wasn't a bad thing for his liver, considering that his life was shattered now and should be swept up with a broom and shoveled into the first garbage bin. Then he saw me in the doorway listening to him, and he quickly changed the topic.

He sits in the arm chair and leans his head of thinning hair against the back rest. Lucio, with rent payment in hand, doesn't know whether to stay or go.

"So, how's it going here?" my father asks him.

"Same as always," I answer.

"Giorgia, how many times do I have to tell you that you ought to wear a suit — jacket and pants — while in the agency?"

35

"I forgot the jacket at home."

My throat is dry. Even if I don't have an aspirator in my mouth sucking up saliva, I feel like I'm at the dentist's. My father rants about western decadence, and Spasimo listens politely.

I turn on the printer, and he interrupts his monologue to tell me: "You've put on some pounds. You should go to the gym, do some jogging…"

I'd like to reply that I'm not like the detectives in American crime fiction, who get up at sunrise to go running on the beach.

"Every ideology disappeared in the Eighties," he resumes.

Spasimo agrees grudgingly.

Then my father gets up, goes to the file cabinet, and opens a row of drawers. He doesn't remember that the bottle of Anisette sits in a compartment of the desk. I see him rack his brains, talking at random so we won't understand what he came here looking for.

I get up too.

"Look at that," he says, "the seat of your pants is almost down to your knees."

Spasimo comes to my aid. "That's the fashion, Major."

Twenty-seven years ago, my mother had honey-colored hair tied back with a clasp, and her brow dripped with sweat. "Giorgia, have you seen my keys?"

"On the table, mama, the round one."

At forty-four, she was still a beautiful woman with ravishingly clear eyes and a long face. I've inherited only her low voice and a fraction of her breast size.

Ada started to scream. From the window I saw the blue light of a police squad car and the red light of an ambulance. From behind, the gray Renault seemed intact, but there was little or nothing left of my mother. I was twelve and I was already broken, like a car that's starting to fall apart. You die with the person who dies. And it takes time to revive.

Fulvio Cantini moves his leg nervously. He has red splotches on his cheeks and deep creases in the sides of his mouth.

"Papa," I say to him, "I don't have time to stay here making small talk, and Spasimo also has work to do…"

"You're following a case?"

"More than one."

"You're doing all right?"

"I'd say so."

"Beware of counting your chickens before they hatch."

I look at Lucio in search of solidarity. Nothing. He's too intent on agreeing with the Major.

"A bird in the hand is worth two in the bush. When my ship comes in…" I grab my purse and jacket. "The bottle you're looking for is there," I add, pointing to the third desk drawer, and then I leave the office.

I have a huge desire to kick my car, but I climb inside and rest my head against the wheel, trying to calm my nerves. I start the engine and begin to drive randomly, no destination in mind, just to relax. The streets are real, the people are real, the trees are real, but I see something else.

I see my father, who speaks to me softly, drawing me aside: "I've told Ada that her mama has had an accident. You're younger, but you take after me…you're strong…"

I see Ada seated at the piano. She turns to me and says: "Did you know that mama had another man?"

After Ada's death, our old two-story house was sold, and I always try not to pass in front of it. When I happen to find myself in that part of town, I speed up and with my eyes scan the bars, the shops, and the thousand other things of my former life. It was a large house, furnished in a sober and functional style, where my mother, on rainy mornings, used to listen to records of Brel and Ferré at full volume. My father never allowed us to have a dog, a cat, or a goldfish. He used to say that animals die before we do, and when they go, everyone feels bad.

At 11:45, I am still in the car, in the parking lot of the restaurant La Lucciola, spying on Mrs. Comolli and her lover seated at their usual table. I'm lost in other thoughts, with the tenth Camel of the day between my lips, when I hear a hand beating against the passenger side window.

The person who climbs inside without asking my permission is an androgynous and skeletal girl: she can't be more than eighteen years old, angular face and short black hair, dress and make-up like a Goth kid from the Eighties.

"What do you want?" I shout.

She points to the woman you can see through the glass window, and raising an arm as thin as a match stick, she makes all her bracelets jangle. "I'm her daughter."

I take a minute to process this fact and then relax.

"Did your father send you"?

"No, he doesn't know I'm here."

Her voice, despite her tough demeanor, is high and childlike.

"You've started tracking your mother?"

She lights up a Philip Morris Extra Light. "Oh, this affair's been going on for two years."

"So you know everything?"

She looks at me amazed. "I thought you were smarter."

"Excuse me, but do you know me?"

"I've seen you around…ever since my father added you to the cast…"

"The cast? But we're not on TV."

I roll down the window to air out the car. "I'm sorry that your mother…"

"My father only cares about money," she interrupts. "That man" — she indicates the boyfriend of her mother — "is a partner of Papa's. It would be much easier now for my father to tell them both to go to hell."

The two lovers leave the restaurant, and the girl bends down under the dashboard so she won't be seen. I have enough photos. I think about putting the Nikon back in the case. I let the Mercedes leave, and after a while I start moving, too.

"How did you get here?" I ask.

"A taxi."

I feel awkward. "Where do you want me to take you?"

"Wherever you're going is fine with me. My name is Gaia," she adds. "My surname you already know."

"Listen, Gaia, I have things to get done."

"Okay, then drop me off at the Certosa."

Obviously, I have to ask her why she wants to be taken to the cemetery. "Excuse me, what are you planning to do at the Certosa?"

"Do you know Byron? He used to go there. He would talk to the grave diggers. He always kept a skull on his table, you know, for inspiration..."

She sits up straight, with her hands on her knees and the amused look of someone who feels strange and rejected. She may be crazy, but I like her.

"Oh, Byron..." I reflect out loud. "Do you want to be a writer?"

"I don't know. As a little girl I used to write — all the time. Three page stories. One story was about a family in which everyone died, but the finest one was titled "Cory and Her Dog." The dog drowned and so did Cory trying to save him. All my characters died, I don't know why."

I scratch my forehead, thinking that Ingeborg Bachmann, my favorite writer, used to say that writing is solitude, isolation, dissatisfaction. "Listen, I'll get you something to eat, then take you home."

I stop the car in front of a tiny bar, more a small market than anything. We go inside. I take a cream-filled pastry from the glass case, and I start to eat it ravenously.

"You're not getting anything?" I ask.

She leans against the freezer case full of ice cream confections. "I never eat."

"Not even a Coca-Cola?"

She signals *no*, while staring at me non-stop.

"I adore eating," I challenge her.

"Evidently."

"Oh, I get it. You don't feel like putting on weight."

"That's not it really," she clarifies. "I don't feel like living."

If it's true that things never happen by chance, the anguish I've felt for the last few days reaches its peak in the clearing on the hill where I've parked the Citroën. I thought that seeing Bologna from above and chatting a bit would do her some good, but the daughter of engineer Comolli has rummaged through my music cassettes and found a collection of Luigi Tenco, which she puts in the player.

As I smoke and look at the beautiful homes of wealthy Bolognesi, she sings "One Day After Another," showing she knows all the words by heart. I don't believe my ears: "One day after another, life goes on. Tomorrow will be a day like yesterday. The ship has already left the port and from the shore it seems a distant point..."

I can't resist: "Why don't you listen to Marilyn Manson like other people your age?"

She hunches her shoulders and opens up her black-painted eyes. "Is it because I dress like this?"

"At a certain age, what you wear is important, or isn't it?"

At last I see her smile and discover that she has beautiful white teeth and dimples.

Before taking her home, I stop by the agency, leave her on Lucio's sofa, and go into my office to download the photos onto my PC. While I plug the cable into the computer, I hear her ask where the bathroom is and then shut herself inside.

I go back to Spasimo's office.

"It's not professional to drive around a client's daughter," he tells me.

"She has some problems."

Lucio shakes his head. "Ah, you attract all the desperate cases..."

"Speaking of desperate cases, is Tim in the neighborhood?"

"He came by earlier and collapsed on the sofa. But how many joints can you smoke? He downed two bottles of water in a second."

"Now he's planning to put a group together."

"But if he doesn't know how to play anything?"

"He says it's not important." At that moment Gaia reappears. "It's nice here," she says.

Spasimo and I look at her perplexed.

We get into the car again, but the daughter of Engineer Comolli won't consider the notion of going back to her house. If she had just a crumb of hunger, I'd take her to a McDonald's. Instead I have the bright idea of heading for the Piazza Verdi Bar, where Tim and his friends are having drinks at this hour.

During the drive, Gaia turns her head toward the passenger window, passes a hand over her face, and rubs it so hard it gets red. I lift my eyes to the six o'clock sky, purple like a bruise, and then examine the strange creature sitting next to me. "Tell me about your parents."

She sighs. "My father thinks money can buy everything, including people."

I slow down, searching for a place to park. "And your mother?"

She shrugs her shoulders, and I don't have time to go into it. I find a free space and ask her to get out of the car. As I turn the wheel, she tilts her head and gives me a piercing stare. "Your headlight is broken," she says.

We go inside the Piazza Verdi Bar, and as soon as they meet, I realize that these two will not get along. Tim returns to his friends after shooting me a glance that says: "And who's this alien?"

She looks around uncomfortably. "I always get the feeling I'm out of sync with everything."

I order a pint of beer. "Gaia, Tim is just a young asshole, and you're too grown up for him."

"Didn't you say he's twenty-three?"

"I meant…that you're more mature."

"Have you ever read Pavese?" she blurts out, giving a look of disgust at the bowl of peanuts on the counter.

"In my youth."

"And Woolf? Plath? Mayakovsky?"

I'm uneasy. "Am I wrong or did they all kill themselves?" I drink my beer in one gulp. "Come on, I'm taking you home."

I move away from the bar and see her pause in alarm. "We don't stop seeing each other now, do we?" she says, mumbling her words.

The only thing I can do is write down the number of her cell phone on the bar receipt.

Fifteen minutes later, I enter the house and run towards the ringing telephone. It's Gigi Marini.

"Are you free this evening?"

"What do you have in mind?"

He sniggers. "I'll explain when I see you."

He takes it the wrong way. "Gigi," I say, taking off my jacket, "Do you know how many ages it's been since I've had an orgasm?"

Moment of silence. "Ah, so the other night then?…"

"It's not that I didn't like it…However, if you're asking if it's your fault…"

He interrupts me quickly. "No, I'm not asking you."

"Fine," I say. "I'll call you when I have a moment."

Then it's Tim's turn to call. "Who was that ugly crow?"

"Tone it down. She's a very smart girl. And she's a lot like you."

"In what way?"

I needle him. "She hasn't yet decided whether to be a rock star, a video clip director, or a fashion photographer."

"You'll be pleased to know," he defends himself, "that I'm studying for an exam."

"Big news, Tim. What exam is it?"

"Theatre history. I'm kicking ass over Brecht and Piscator. Political theatre, you know…"

"Ah, political theatre…" I have too much fun pulling his leg when he takes on that know-it-all tone. "So that means I'll have to do without your Spy Cam for a bit."

"I'll lend it to you, but don't even think of getting rid of me."

I smile. "Anything else?"

"Where did you find this girl?"

"She's the daughter of Comolli."

"Fuck, so she's loaded!"

"Now that you know, you'll take her to the movies?"

"I don't think so… She's an ugly little thing… Well, no, Fede says she's not bad, but she's so dark…"

"She has a problem."

"Such as?"

"She doesn't eat."

"First year of high school I saw a girl fade away like that. She wanted to be a model."

"I don't believe that's the case with Gaia."

I say goodbye to Tim, toss the cordless phone on the sofa, and the first thing I see is the shoe box on the little end table. I take off my boots, sit on the arm rest, and grab some pages…

January 10, 1986

It's a world of promises and no results, Aldo. I hope things are going better with you than they are with me. At every audition I see streams of actors ready for everything: modern gladiators, prepared for combat despite missing an arm and an eye. Without blood, there is no spectacle…

I hold the box in my hands: there are envelopes inside I still haven't opened. Tonight, however, I'm too tired.

It was a November evening in 1977, and Ada and I had just left the Teatro Duse after seeing *Cyrano de Bergerac* with Pino Micol. We went back to the house on foot — a half hour walk — and we didn't manage to talk: our emotions were too strong.

"Do you understand? This is what I want to do."

I nodded, hugging myself in my blue overcoat with a sense of fear. At fifteen, it was already decided: Ada would become an actress, and I a lawyer.

Ever since that evening, there were so many shows she dragged me to see: *Leonce e Lena* with Antonio Salines at the Teatro Testoni, *The Man with the Luggage* by Ionesco with Tino Buazzelli, *The Power of Darkness* by Tolstoy with Sbragia and Placido, *Measure for Measure* with Lavia, Vannucchi, Scaccia, and Piccolo…until the time when, seated on stage, at the end of *Richard III*, she fell in love with Carmelo Bene and began to cut out all of his newspaper photos and read his books.

I wasn't like her. The world weighed on me. I protested in the piazza against the neo-fascist Almirante, I went to meetings of the communist youth group, I danced with comrades in the ballroom of the Grieco headquarters at their membership drive party, I spoke about youth movements at the Piccolo Bar in Via Toscana, and I went to the Palazzo dello Sport to hear Dalla sing "How Deep Is the Sea."

Papa bought her a scooter, a white Ciao, that was stolen one day in front of Liceo Fermi, and Ada began to go to the theatre by herself. We never spoke about our mother. Just the mention of her made me break up inside like a window pane, and I believe the same thing was true of her. We started to realize somewhat, my sister and I, that the dead don't come back, and also to realize somewhat just how present they are, sometimes more than the living.

I remember one evening in May. It was 1978. I remember it well because Moro had been killed a week earlier. Later on, the World Cup would begin in Argentina, and in July Sandro Pertini would be elected President of the Republic after the ouster of Leone. Ada and I had just left the Embassy Theatre: we had seen *Saturday Night Fever*, and we began dancing in the middle of the street imitating John Travolta.

Suddenly, she stopped goofing around and told me that she felt a kind of remorse that would not go away. When I asked her what she meant, she replied that Mama's accident had something to do with it. I don't know why, but I had this fear. I stood there without knowing what to say. At home we crawled into bed, in the dark, to listen to "Liu" by the Alunni del Sole and "Losing Anna" by Tozzi.

But all this happened later. After the death of Ilaria Maggi in Cantini...

On Christmas Eve of 1975, our mother took us to Midnight Mass. Mama already had those restless eyes, pupils that never stopped moving. I remember her hands in black leather gloves and her skinny body inside a fur coat much too large for her. A year later, in the same church, the day of her funeral, I saw a man greet my father with a nod and then cover his face with his hands. Aunt Lidia, my papa's sister, said, "Doesn't he have a lot of nerve to show up here?"

From that day, Ada began to steal money from Papa's wallet to buy small packs of Mercedes cigarettes. She smoked in the bathroom, secretly, with the window wide open. When I heard the toilet flush, I knew she was putting out the butt, and she would spray her throat with Tantum Verde. The day that Papa discovered her, he grounded her for a week. I see her again on our bedroom rug, cutting out photos of Claudia Marsani, the fifteen-year old chosen by Visconti for *Conversation Piece*, and the photo in which a very young Tatum O'Neal receives an Oscar for *Paper Moon* from the hands of Charles Bronson.

I take the bottle of Four Roses from the side table, attack it, drain it, and go to sleep, still dressed, on the sofa. At eight in the morning, I'm still in this position. I sleep for five or six hours, then open my eyes again, and the same totally banal and shitty reality is still there. I get up from the sofa, a crumpled mess. I need a coffee and a cigarette really bad.

I had just gotten into my car when I see my young colleague beating his fist against the window.

"I'm coming with you," he says, tossing his helmet and backpack onto the backseat.

I speed up as if I'm in a big hurry. Tim takes out the tools of his trade and starts to roll a joint.

Thirty or so dusty cassette tapes are bouncing around under his seat. He lifts up one by chance. *Please Don't Go* by KC and the Sunshine Band put me in a good mood.

Almost all of my cassettes, sliding from side to side on the floor mats of the car at every turn or brake, are new-wave music.

Tim, drawing out one tape after another, looks at them with curiosity.

"Who is this Blondie?"

"Ah, Debbie Harry, the queen of the underground. Ever heard of 'Call Me'?"

He shakes his head.

"It was the theme song of *American Gigolo*. You've seen that for sure."

"Maybe. I've heard people talk about Devo. They did a cover of 'I Can't Get No Satisfaction.'"

"Wonderful."

"And Joy Division?"

"I ought to have *Disorder*. Look around for it…"

He grabs another cassette. "I do know Bauhaus. The bass part to "Bela Lugosi's Dead" is mythic, right?"

"I adore Peter Murphy's voice. It's so deep. And Daniel Ash's guitar playing…wild."

He shows admiration. "You're really an expert."

"No, but I followed music closely in those years."

"That is, when you were young."

"We all have a youth. Then it goes, Tim. Even yours will pass."

He pretends he didn't hear anything. "The Residents?"

"Without a doubt, the best of all."

"Is this the only way to see you smile?"

I give him a questioning look.

"You only get enthusiastic when you talk about music."

I park the car in the parking lot of the Esse Lunga, the company where Alfio Tolomelli works. "Come on, Tim, grab your Nikon. It's time to go to work."

"What's the story with this guy"

"He's doing it with his wife's cousin. You see that car? I point my finger at a small blue Fiat 500. That's Maria Veronesi's car."

"The cousin."

"Maybe she's come to find him at his lunch break." I show him a picture. "That's her in the middle with the pony tail and the red dress. The brunette is Lucia Tolomelli."

We weave in and out of mothers pushing their baby carriages and shopping carts full of groceries. Then at a bar deep in the shopping district, in front of a retail sports store, we run into the two of them seated at a table. Maria Veronesi, a curly-haired woman in her thirties with broad shoulders and ample waist, supports her chin sadly with one hand; Alfio Tolomelli, bull-neck and rock-climber legs, caresses her hair consolingly, while he moves around a pile of cigarette butts with his pointy suede boot.

Tim, hidden behind an escalator, shoots twenty or so pictures. When we climb back into the car, he asks, "How do you tell this to his wife?"

"The usual way. Lucia Tolomelli pays me to find out the truth. And the truth is tactless, however you say it."

The radio plays a piece by 99 Posse, and I look outside with disgust.

"Does it always have to rain? Is it possible? Rain should be more reserved…more of a rare event, for us to appreciate it."

Tim lowers the volume. The wipers squeak. "Look, it's not raining anymore."

In front of my house, before getting out of the car, I remember that he and his sister Fiorenza are having a party.

"You know I don't care for parties," I fume, bent over the wheel.

He tries to convince me. "Look, it's not just kids, but friends of Fiori, too, and a couple of my teachers."

"Then I really can't miss it."

"If you also want to bring what's-her-name, the Christina Ricci look-alike…"

"Her name is Gaia, and she's a very lonely girl."

"Ah," he says, "your maternal instinct has sprung into action?"

"Go fuck yourself, Tim."

CHAPTER 4

For the party at Tim's house, I wear a pair of khaki colored trousers I keep for the rare social events I attend. Gaia, instead, has on a sleeveless black, high-neck sweater and tight jeans. Her large dark eyes are made up like the 1920s, and her shiny black lips are like two nervous scribbles on a milk-white face.

Fiorenza meets us with a smile, thanks me for the bottle of Sangiovese, and ushers us into a living room full of rugs, sofas, and modern paintings on the walls. The room is crowded, and in the background you can hear Coldplay. On a piano-shaped glass table, bottles of liquor, trays of canapes, and bowls of olives and pistachios.

Fiorenza works in an art gallery. She has coal-black hair, almond eyes, and a face tanned by the Balearic sun, where she's recently been on vacation. The guests go back and forth between the glass table and another one, full of sushi, balanced on a trestle table. A staircase leads to a platform where Tim has placed his camera. I see him walking down the steps with bags under his eyes, a faded sweatshirt, and his usual jeans.

"Hi," he says to me and Gaia in the tone of someone who just woke up from a late afternoon nap, then he plops down onto a sofa with his feet on the arm rest.

I look around.

In one corner, there's a girl in a pin-striped suit talking to the director of a local newspaper. Another woman, a friend of Fiorenza, has the straight-line body of an adolescent, even though she's over forty. (I sigh with envy in her direction.) Seated on a Persian carpet is Viola, the blonde girl that Tim and Fede have been quarreling over for the past few weeks.

I'm immediately aware of him. He's turned aside and talking to a woman in her thirties, who wears a pair of shoes with heels as long and thin as Chinese chopsticks. He holds her brightly colored cloth purse so she can refill her glass, then gives it back to her. Our looks meet.

He has narrow, clear eyes and wears a corduroy jacket. He takes a seat on a folding aluminum chair, next to a boy who spends a lot of time in the gym, and they start talking about things that must not interest him very much.

"I do ten reps at a time," the boy says, "then I do some crunches for the abs..."

When I turn to the table to eat something, I find him next to me, intent on sniffing the cork of a bottle of cabernet he just opened. Under his brown jacket, he wears a dark gray, V-neck sweater, and his large face is marked by bags under his eyes that I hadn't noticed from a distance.

He smiles at me. "Andrea, a pleasure to meet you."

"A friend of Fiorenza?"

He has a lilting voice with soft, light *r*'s. "No, of Timothy. I'm his history of film teacher. And you, baby?"

Skip the fact that we're more or less the same age, skip the fact that we're at a party, but who gave him permission to address me in such a familiar way? Perhaps he's a sensitive type, for he corrects himself quickly. "Can we call each other by our first names?"

"Certainly," I concede with clenched teeth. "So, does this cabernet have a corky smell?"

"No, it's perfect," he says, pouring some in a glass for me.

I turn to look for Gaia. She's sitting on a sofa, legs folded beneath her, as Tim passes her a joint. I stumble and almost turn a trivet over, but the professor has good reflexes and manages to catch it in midair.

"Are you going to take off your jacket?" he asks.

"I don't believe I'll be staying for very long."

"Another engagement?"

"I don't like parties."

He scrutinizes me closely, and I must say, despite the chill his blue eyes instill in me, Andrea Berti has a penetrating look.

"What's the matter?"

He shifts his gaze elsewhere. "Excuse me, but I get the feeling that I've seen you before."

"Do you have a light?" I ask him.

"Sorry, but I don't smoke."

There are two types of men I can't stand: the ones without a driver's license and the ones who don't smoke.

"That is," he clarifies, "I stopped years ago."

"That's something I could never do."

"It's not so hard, and it's better for your health. All in all, you live longer."

"Not everyone wants to live longer." A cutting answer that Gaia would like.

"Are you always so brusque?"

"Brusque is my second name."

Here's why I hate parties. Even if you're an intelligent person, you tend to sound like a cretin among other cretins.

"What's your name? Seriously."

"Giorgia."

"Ah, now I know who you are. Tim has spoken to me about you…"

The woman with high heels comes up to him. "Andrea, how is your assistant doing?"

"Luisa Artieri? She's fine, but now she's on maternity leave, and we don't often see each other."

Andrea Berti turns toward me again, and she goes off with a grimace of disappointment. I'm not used to being the object of a man's attention, and it makes me nervous.

"May I tell you a joke?"

"Only if it's dirty."

My aggressive manner turns him on. Perhaps he's asking himself if it's a seduction tactic.

"I don't know if it's up to your standard."

"Then you better not tell it to me."

He studies me with a half-smile. "What would you like to talk about?"

"Frankly, I'd just like to drink. After all, I'm at a party."

"Cop movies are full of women like you."

"What sort of women?"

"Hard on themselves and on the opposite sex."

I play along. "Daughters of cops who work in a chauvinistic environment and struggle to gain a bit of respect?"

"You're all right."

"Thanks."

He turns to greet someone, and so I go over to Gaia and tell her I'm bored, even though it's not true. As we stand in the doorway, ready to leave, saying goodbye to Fiorenza, who insists that we stay, I notice Andrea Berti smiling at me. I see him come leaping toward us down the carpeted hallway, almost running into an iron sculpture. "I hope we'll see each other again," he says.

"For sure," I say.

"Is that a promise?"

I flash a polite smile and take my leave.

On the stairway, Gaia asks me: "Do you think you'll see him again?"

"No."

"But you promised him!"

"Oh, people promise lots of things when they're drunk."

"That's also true when they're sober."

I look at her admiringly.

I have a vague memory of where I parked the Citroën. All I know is that it's far from here, but I'm not concerned. I light a cigarette and offer one to Gaia.

We walk slowly, enjoying the lanes and little side streets.

"At one time this was the most popular avenue with rich people," I tell her as we enter the Strada Maggiore, "and it's not too different nowadays. Here's where your friend Lord Byron lived for a while…"

"I know," she says proudly, then lowers her head and reflects. "It's crazy," she says.

"What?"

"Here, right where we're strolling, a bunch of people passed by who've been dead for ages. An entire lifetime of people we don't know, who loved and suffered just like us…"

I open my arms.

"What's left, Giorgia? Yes, what trace do we leave behind?"

I crush out a butt end and don't know what to answer. We pass in front of a club that just opened up, the kind of place where they press a drink card in your hand as soon as you enter. I turn up my nose, and Gaia observes it. "And the famous Bologna taverns?"

"Not many are left anymore, but years and years ago they were the true university. Places where you talked about everything, poetry, war…just like in the brothels."

"The brothels?"

"The female senator Merlin shut them down in 1958. Lamentation all the way from Via Zamboni to Via Bertiera. It was like the end of civilization when they closed the doors on Via delle Oche…"

Gaia arches her eyebrows. "You weren't around then."

"These are stories that my father used to tell me."

"Did he visit the whorehouses?"

I burst into laughter. "No, he's not the type."

"Who knows how many writers were born there?…"

"In the brothels? It's possible." I stop in front of my Citroën and rest my elbows on the wet, dirty car roof. "I'd like to read the stuff you've written."

She smiles embarrassed. "It's mainly poetry."

"Ah," I swallow, "I like poetry."

"Have you ever heard of Anubis?"

I look for my car keys in my purse. "The god with a man's body and a jackal's head, right? In eighth grade I had a passion for the ancient Egyptians…"

"He was the guardian of the tombs and accompanied the deceased to Osiris, the god of the dead."

"Sure, the god of the dead."

"But my favorite is the goddess Hathor...the Greeks call her Aphrodite..."

"Hmm."

"In their drawings she's represented as a cow with a body full of stars."

I open the car door. "Is that how you feel about yourself?"

She lowers her eyes. No, it's how I imagine my mother."

I drive slowly behind a garbage truck and who knows how many Smart Cars.

As Gaia lights me a cigarette, I reflect on the protective feeling this girl inspires in me. She starts in on another of her obsessions, the one she has for Amazons. She's written a short poem about them called "Armor-Plates." She mentions a certain Hippolyta, who could wield the bow and the spear, and had her breast cut off as a little girl so she could do it even better. She explains to me that the word Amazon means "woman of the moon" and that men just considered them pieces of shit who hated males. "But they were the sort who sought for equality between the sexes," she tells me. And then Penthesilea, whom Achilles was madly in love with, and who could tame the wildest horses...

"Gaia," I interrupt, "why did you say yesterday that you have no desire to live."

She puts a finger between her teeth, with her head against the door window. "Have you ever lost someone?"

"Two gold medals in that category. And you?..."

She stares at me, a bit resentfully. "Do I seem too young to have already lost someone?"

I think of myself at her age. "No."

"And that I don't seem to have much sense..."

"What are you talking about?"

"To be or not to be...you get it, right?"

I decide to take her seriously. "When my sister hanged herself, I was six years older than you. If you need someone to explain to you why, all in all, it's better to breathe, then I'm here for you. But if that crap is part of your future plans, I'm telling you right off, don't come looking for me anymore."

I stop the car outside the front gate to the Comolli's villa. Gaia gets out, head lowered, with a dark and pensive expression. Before she shuts the door, I tell her: "'Think it over,' Gaia."

She closes her eyes with a nod.

I smile at her. "It's a Lou Reed song."

Then I go back home.

The first thing I do, after slipping into my pajamas and turning off the cell phone, is to organize the letters scattered on the living room table: an operation I carry out mechanically, without thought, until something falls out of an envelope… I bend over to pick it up. In the photo, my sister has on a cherry-red bra and a flowery robe cinched at the waist; her tanned face smiles at the camera lens. Embracing her is a swarthy and muscular boy, with a mole on his left cheek: Aldo.

There's writing on the back: "Summer 1985. I don't regret it. Love, Ada."

At 11:10 pm, I grab the phone and a voice answers me in English that Aldo isn't there. I leave a message for him to call me back as soon as he returns. I sit on a stool in the kitchen and drink a can of Heineken.

Finally, at 11:35, Aldo himself calls. I ask my question, and I hear him breathe like someone just coming up for air. "Listen, Giorgia, that summer…"

"I'm all ears."

"We went to that island of Giglio, remember? You didn't want to come…"

"But Giulio was there."

"Yes, he was."

"Go on."

"Only if you stop it with that prison-guard tone."

I want to scream. "Aldo, don't make me lose my patience."

"It was just…a fling between Ada and me."

"You're a shit."

"Let me finish."

"And you call the friendship you've had since nursery school a fling?"

"It was just lust."

I'm beside myself. "Sure, why not. A nice incestuous fuck!"

Silence. Neither of us dares to speak. I'm about to hang up, when I hear him say: "When she came back to Rome with Giulio, we started writing each other. I know you can't understand… Neither of us knew why it happened, but that night brought us together…"

"I ask you for the last time. Who was A.?"

"I swear on Ada, I don't know."

I walk up and down the living room with my head splitting open and a lit Camel between my fingers. I open the address book, pick up the cordless phone, and dial Giulio's number.

Seven years ago, Giulio Manfredini, Ada's ex, was transferred to Milan. The last time I spoke to him was a year ago, when his son Enrico was born. (I ask myself if he's changed, if he has those same curls that dangle over his eyes like tropical vines, if he's put on weight, and if he still gets fired up talking about politics.) He answers after a few rings, and I ask him right away to excuse me for calling so late. I hear a baby crying in the background and the voice of Nicoletta, his wife, trying to calm him down.

Giulio seems glad to hear my voice.

"Pardon me, but I've been reading some old letters of Ada's, and I asked myself if you…" I can't find the words. "Giulio, how were things going between you two?"

"Stay on the line; I'm going into another room."

A bit later, I hear his voice again. "Ada and I hadn't been making love for a while. She was very depressed because of her work, and she was confiding in a new friend…"

"Which friend?"

"Anna. She also went to the funeral, remember?"

No, I don't remember. "There were so many people. What do you know about her?"

"Giorgia, your voice is…I'm busy right now."

"Giulio," I insist. "What do you know about her?"

"Well, that she liked women."

I register this and move on to pleasantries. "How's Enrico?"

"He's a fantastic baby. You should come visit us…"

I crush out the cigarette in the can. Aldo answers at the first ring. Perhaps he was waiting for me to call him back.

"Aldo."

His voice sounds softer. "Yes, I'm here."

"How's life going for you over there?"

"I've finished writing my fifth unpublished book, and I'm reviewing other people's books for a magazine, then some more translation…"

"Are you with anyone?"

"Now and then."

Aldo Cinelli. I still remember how he liked to fill the world with questions to keep others from asking about his own life. The girls always steered him away from his own aspirations. Living dangerously through romantic difficulties, always without a dime in his pocket, always with a backpack on his shoulders, and a French, German, or English dictionary.

I go straight to the point. "Tell me what you know. Please."

"Wait while I get a cigarette."

He's back after a few seconds. "Ada wanted to leave Giulio, Rome, and all the rest… She was tired, depressed, and had begun drinking."

I open the fridge, take out another can, and pull hard on the tab.

"Naturally, she didn't want your father to know."

"Naturally. And A.?"

"She had gone crazy over him."

"Was she pregnant?"

Silence.

"I don't know."

"Did A. beat her?"

"Well, if you drink and you snort coke… Sometimes that will happen."

"Did she ever talk to you about suicide?"

"Not about her own."

(I know who he's referring to: my mother.)

"Did she ever speak to you about a certain Anna?"

A slight pause. "I don't believe so."

"Aldo…did Ada also like women?"

I feel him take his time. "Let it go. It's the past."

I lose my grip. "It's my past."

He becomes protective. "Why do you still want to hurt yourself?"

Silence.

"Giorgia, I'm going to give you some advice."

"Brotherly advice?"

He doesn't take the hint. "Let the dead rest and worry about the living. How's your father doing?"

"Good night, Aldo."

CHAPTER 5

After another restless night, I wake up in a foul mood with my right eye even more inflamed. If I were someone who puts on makeup, I'd try to camouflage the difference between one eye and the other. I place the lit cigarette on the edge of the sink, wash my face, pick up the cigarette again, blink my eyes, and breathe in.

Looking in the mirror, I think of myself at sixteen, the ambulance in front of the house, and my sister on the wooden bench. "You say she's dead already?"

Half an hour later, we were brought into an unknown reality. The hospital. The aunt who was saying: "It's here where you're born, and it's here where you die."

My god, I'm tired of being human, tired of it. I put out the cigarette under the faucet, rub some toothpaste on my teeth, then leave the house.

My only contact with the police goes by the name of Bruni: Luca Bruni, forty-six, married, one son, the chief of police for Bologna. I got to know him years ago while I followed the case of Giulia Manzoni, and I've had occasion to appreciate both his human and his professional qualities. Then, as often happens, we lost sight of each other, knowing we could count on each other if we needed to. I'm inside a bookstore on Via Orti, in front of the paperbacks on a turning display case, when my cell phone rings and it's him. He asks me if I've read the papers, and when I say "No," he tells me to stay where I am. He'll be there soon. He needs to speak to me, urgently.

I leave the bookstore and walk up and down in front of a two-story house, with a tiled walkway bordered by rectangular cement flower beds. It's time for a cigarette, and Bruni gets out of his blue Opal, greeting me with a curt movement of his head.

He has a tired and drawn face, short gray hair, and eyes that look straight at you without suggestion. Instinct and experience are one and the same in him. He's a man who can live with all the decisions he makes, including their consequences. His tall thin body exudes moral equilibrium from all its pores.

He's not the type to waste time with "How's it going?" "Donatella Verze. Does that name mean anything to you?"

I shrug my shoulders.

"She's getting separated from Giordano Lattice. It appears, from some documents found at his house, that he's a client of yours."

"Sure," I start to panic, "sure, he's a client of mine! He still has to pay me, that bastard!"

Bruni offers me a coffee at a nearby bar. My legs turn to putty while he informs me that two days ago Donatella Verza was found strangled in her apartment on Via Marsala.

I'm speechless, shaken by the news, but then I begin to tell him my impressions of Giordano Lattice: his jealousy towards his wife, my photos that attest to the many boyfriends she spent her time with. At the end I shake my head. "He has a leg in a cast. I don't think that…"

"People take off their casts," Bruni interrupts me, "provided their legs are broken for real."

I gulp down the coffee, burning my palate. "What do you know?"

"The night Mrs. Verze died, he was playing poker with friends."

"And you believe him?" (Idiotic question: Bruni never believes anyone.)

"I need to see the photos," he tells me.

We leave the bar, and Bruni opens his car door to take me to the agency to pick them up. Fastening the seatbelt, however, I remember that I put them in an envelope to give to Lattice: the photos are in the glove compartment of the Citroën.

A few minutes later, I hand Bruni the envelope and say goodbye, asking him to keep me up to date.

I arrive at the agency mulling things over and promising to read the paper for more information, then I'm startled by the sight of the Major sitting in the leather arm chair of the office, now more mine than his.

"Hi, I was waiting for you." He looks at me. "Did you have a bad night's sleep?"

I stare at him so long that he looks away and nods at a bill that I haven't paid.

"Papa, today's not a work day…"

"So?"

"So we can talk about Ada."

"What?"

"You heard me. Ada!"

He fidgets in the chair, clutching the lapel of the brown overcoat that he still hasn't removed. I open the desk drawer, take out the bottle of Anisette, and bang it down on the table top, elbowing aside papers, pens, and envelopes full of photos. "Are you thirsty?"

He directs his eyes towards a crumpled piece of paper fallen from the waste basket and adopts a tone of confidence. "I should never have let her leave and throw herself into a city like that, so full of competition. I should have kept her here in the province."

I stare at him as he stares at the Anisette.

"Did Ada know about Mama?

"In what sense?"

I corner him. "That it wasn't an accident."

"Listen, Giorgia…they're going to turn off the lights soon."

I fling my purse to the ground. "Fine, I'll stay in the dark. Answer me!"

He moves his head from side to side and stares at the cracks in the ceiling. "I don't want to talk about it yet."

"But we've never talked about it, ever!"

He can't bring himself to look me in the eyes. "She found out afterwards…"

I stare at him open-mouthed for a few moments, and I know that not a word will escape me. As I leave the office, I catch a glimpse of my father lifting his arm towards the bottle.

"You're not one to cry, are you?" Ada screamed at me the day our mother died. She was wearing a pink cotton night-shirt, edged in velvet, with a bright pink ribbon on the collar. She had just left my father's ground-floor office, which is crammed with books on World War II, medals of valor, and a framed photograph on the wall of Alcide de Gasperi, the founder of the Christian Democratic Party. I watched her, stunned by her pure rage, and I felt just like the glass case where Papa used to keep his guns. Ada didn't stop sobbing, crouched in a corner of the bed; sooner or later I thought she'd calm down, just as she did one Christmas a few years earlier, when they had given her a doll that immediately broke, and she started to yell so loudly that Papa closed all the windows, saying: "It's clear you really didn't want it — otherwise, it wouldn't have fallen."

But now it was all about Mama, who used to smile with a far-away-look, toward a distant point, with an expression so lost and vague that I thought she was talking with ghosts.

(That expression passed directly as an inheritance to my sister, unconsciously or by imitation.)

I remember, while she wept, I turned my gaze towards the wall with a little oil painting of kittens in a basket. I remember that at a certain point Ada wiped her face with the edge of the muslin curtain. I remember that my lips were dry and that it was pouring rain outside. I remember that I felt inadequate, planted there in the doorway, with my cheeks drawn into an idiotic half-smile.

I pick out Serena Battaglia, the fiancée of Alvise Lumini, sitting at the small table of a bar that serves first courses and salads. She's reading a newspaper with a glass of café macchiato in front of her. She's thin, subdued, and looks older than twenty-nine, perhaps because of the bags under her eyes and her unwashed blonde hair. I ask myself what a robust fellow, bursting with health like Alvise Lumini, is doing with her.

The table next to hers is free, so I sit down and order a cappuccino. I watch her intently until she becomes aware of me. "Would you like the paper?" she asks politely.

"Oh," I say, "I'll wait till you're done."

She folds the paper and hands it to me. "I've already read it."

Her café macchiato must be cold. "Check!" she shouts at a waiter moving among the tables.

I turn the pages until I reach the local news section, and I get depressed looking at the photos of Donatella Verze that don't do justice to her beauty. I come back to reality, and I try to make up something. "How crazy," I say. "They announced that someone died of a heart attack, and then he wakes up."

"This is why I wouldn't be cremated. You never know…"

"My name is Giorgia. Giorgia Cantini."

She looks around, a little uneasy. "Well…I'm Serena."

"Truly serene or just a name?"

She appreciates the witticism. "I wouldn't say so."

"Why not? You have such a tranquil manner… Now that I think about it, you have the look of a woman in love."

"Absolutely!" she exclaims, half sarcastic and half dismissive.

"You mean, you're not in love?"

"How about you…are you in love?"

"You've got to be joking. I try to avoid disasters like that."

She laughs as she looks me over. Eyeliner highlights the ghostly gleam in her eyes.

I offer her the pack of Camels. "Do you smoke?"

She hesitates and then takes a cigarette from the pack. "Okay, one smoke and then I'm off. I have a pile of skirts to work on…"

I light her cigarette. "Can we use first names with each other?"

She nods, indecisive, then sizes me up with a frown.

(It's useless. I can't detect the scent of orange blossoms around her.)

"What's your line of work?" she asks.

"I work for the Twin Souls Agency."

She laughs again, crossing her arms on her wool cardigan. "A while back, I could have used it, but now I'm about to get married." She adjusts a lock of hair behind her ear. "He's the one who insists on it. I'm all right with living together. Are you married?"

True to my script, I answer: "I'm a restless spirit. I like messing up my life."

She tosses her head backward. "You say this to…"

"When do you get married?"

"March 4."

"You have plenty of time to change your mind."

She smirks. "With my past, it's a miracle that I've found someone who'll marry me…"

Here comes my favorite phrase. "We all have a past." I see her stiffen. "May I offer you something? A Campari, a Limoncello?" I ask.

"No thanks, I really have to go."

My last opportunity. "I know I've seen you somewhere before…"

Suddenly, Serena Battaglia looks me up and down and, without mincing words, floors me. "Were you a working girl?"

I close my eyes half-way and nod with fake humility.

And she: "In an apartment?"

"Carmen's Salon, the special massage studio."

She rests a hand on the sleeve of my wind breaker. "Listen, let me get you a cappuccino."

I look at her and feel like a piece of shit. "Thanks, Serena."

"What street is your agency on?"

I make up an address on the spot. "Via Sante Vincenzi."

"Perhaps I'll send you an invitation to the wedding."

"I'll be there for sure and…good luck to you."

"Maybe the worst is over," she says, putting on a coat two sizes too large for her.

I smile with clenched teeth. "Maybe."

The sun never shines on Gigiola's apartment, and perhaps for that reason she's decorated it with light-colored furniture that brightens it up a bit. Floor lamps and table lamps are strewn here and there, lit up every hour of the day and night. It's three in the afternoon, and she's just gotten up. She's fifty-years old, and has a round moon-face that she never applies makeup to. You can glimpse her soft body, lounging on a striped sofa, through her half-open dressing gown.

"You ought to come by a bit more often," she scolds me.

I smile and show her the photo of Serena Battaglia. "Do you know her?"

Her little hands grip the photo. Fingers like butterflies tap the bright paper. "Of course I do, this is Serena."

She lifts herself lazily from the sofa to pour herself some whisky. "Are you thirsty?" she asks me, handing back the photo.

I shake my head. "What can you tell me about her?"

She smiles lightly, attentive to the tight pull of her face lift. "A precocious girl. She had fabulous years and then started going with a guy who ruined her. I always say that early success makes a bad ending."

"Did she work in house?"

"She worked everywhere. Absolutely fearless. She confronted everything like an avalanche. In short, she knew how to defend herself. Then she fell in love with a drug dealer, someone who used to beat her. He gave her black eyes... Men like that make you appreciate solitude." She looks away toward the TV, turned on with the volume down low. "They say she was really into kinky sex — *contra naturam*."

She bursts out laughing, and I relax. Every time I'm tired of twisted people I come to Gigiola's. She's right, I ought to visit her more often.

"Do you remember my bus driver? It's been a long time…"

"What happened to him?"

"Oh, he got married. Every time I saw him, I dissolved like aspirin."

She laughs again, as she takes a sip of whiskey. Then she closes her eyes, and her head falls forward. I ask myself if she's gone to sleep, but I hear her hoarse voice murmur: "They say you drink to forget. But what kind of expression is that?… The more I drink, the more I remember."

I tap the cigarette ash into a pink orchid-shaped ashtray.

"The other day, I thought of Giosuè Maccaferri, the only man in the world who wanted to marry me. Hell, he never talked, he had no interests in life, he was a…what do you call it? A tabula rasa. If we had produced a son, I'm sure he would have been a Forrest Gump. Yes, it's much better I didn't marry him."

"I'm investigating Serena."

Gigiola doesn't hear me. She opens her eyes and stares at the TV screen. "What a stupid world, a frenzy of finger-pointing specialists on call. Think about the people who commit murder — the father, the wife — and then comes Mister Know-It-All to explain how things like this happen. But what do we care? Right out here they've written on a wall: 'Erika and Omar and Annamaria Franzoni: 2 to 1,' like a soccer score."

At this point, I also laugh.

"When my grandmother was sick and tired of my grandfather, she took a shovel and split his head in half, like a watermelon. Only a short article in the paper. Well, all right, those were other times. Today she'd be a celebrity."

She turns off the TV with the remote control and sizes me up in silence. "So, Serena…she's gotten out of the business?"

"So it seems. A client of mine wants to marry her."

She leans forward, glass in hand. Her voice is a whisper. "Giorgia, she's someone who calculates. A true whore. You understand me? Even if that asshole marries her, even if everything goes nice and smooth for a while, she'll still go back to the game, because somebody like that always goes back. She keeps returning like a bladder infection."

I get up from the chair. "And how are you doing?"

I see her head sway, indecisive. "A little tired. But I don't complain."

In the doorway, I promise to come by for another visit.

In the agency, Spasimo leaves his bunker with ruffled hair and thick glasses balanced precariously on his nose.

"A certain Marini called," he tells me.

"What did he want?" I ask, taking off my jacket.

He reads a post-it note. "Tell her that tonight I am playing at the Container."

"Ah, are you coming with me?"

"Where?"

"The Container."

He doesn't waste time replying. "And then Davide Melloni called. He was at the bar with Frank and wanted to know if you'd join them for an aperitif."

"Many thanks, Lucio."

"At your service."

Spasimo turns and shuts himself inside his office. I sit at my desk and start up the computer. The telephone rings.

I assume the tone of an efficient secretary: "Cantini Investigative Agency."

"Good morning, my name is Alessandro Dazi," a manly voice announces pleasantly, "and I'd like to make an appointment."

"For when?"

"As soon as possible."

"Who referred you to our agency?"

"No one. I found the number in the phone book."

Obviously, I think. "Ah...is it an urgent matter?"

"Yes."

"Then come right away. Do you know the address?"

Thirty minutes later, I open the door to a man in his forties, dark skin, about six feet tall, brilliant black eyes, and fleshy lips. I catch sight of Spasimo spying from his doorway and motion for him to make himself scarce. I invite Alessandro Dazi to take a seat on the leather arm chair. He takes off his coat and stands there in a dark blue cashmere sweater and perfectly tailored trousers.

"Dr. Cantini," he says as he sits down, "I'm looking for a woman who disappeared."

I like people who go straight to the point, and I don't spoil the mood explaining that I'm not a doctor. "Please…" I invite him to continue.

"Her name is Angela, and I met her years ago in Rome."

My senses are on the alert. "Angela…and her last name?"

"De Santis. I've heard nothing more about her — not for twelve years. The only thing I know is that I'd like to see her again."

"Why?"

He bites his lower lip and sighs like a skilled actor. "Because she's the only woman I've ever loved in my whole life."

I lean against the back of my swivel chair and light a cigarette. "Would you like one?"

"No thanks. May I?" he asks, taking from his pants pocket a box of Davidoffs.

"Certainly."

"Thanks, you're very kind. Not everyone can stand the smell of cigars."

"I'll open the window as soon as you leave."

He smiles. Straight, gleaming white teeth.

"What information can you give me?"

"The address of the house where she used to live with other people."

"How did you lose contact with her?"

"My fault entirely. I was about to marry."

"And did you get married?"

"Twice."

"Now you're a free man?"

"Yes, I live alone in an apartment downtown, I see my three children on the weekend, and I work like a madman to pay alimony to my ex-wives."

"A lousy life," I say.

His tone is firm. "Yes."

I scribble on a piece of paper without looking up. "And so, you lived in Rome?..."

"Yes, I did my military service. Then I stayed there to work as a window dresser to pay for my studies."

"What subject did you study?"

"I didn't finish college. However, I was enrolled in economics and marketing."

I raise my head. "Have you ever acted?"

"No, never. But who wouldn't want to be an actor?"

"I, for one." I pass the ashtray to him. "Are you sure?"

"Of what?"

"That you've never been an actor?"

He crosses his legs and taps the ashes. "I'm certainly sure of it."

"You've never even tried your hand at it?"

He rubs the tip of his perfect nose with his finger. (A cocaine user?) "Well, I started out as an extra in a few films to make a little money. You know how it is in Rome. Two out of three people you meet are actors or would like to be..."

"Yes...and Angela De Santis?"

"She studied psychology."

"Are you sure?"

He fidgets in the chair. "Why do you always ask me if I'm sure?"

"It's my job."

"All right, excuse me. At the time...Angela wanted to be a singer."

"Did she cut a record?"

He removes an invisible strand of hair from his sweater. "I don't believe so."

I hand him a note pad. "Write down addresses, names of people who knew her, telephone numbers, everything that can be useful to me. I'll leave you just for a minute."

I go out of the room and take some air. A. Alessandro. Dazi. He lived in Rome and had some walk-on parts… Spasimo sees me bang my head against the glass door of the bathroom.

"What are you doing?"

I motion for him to lower his voice. "It could be him…"

"Which him?"

"Ada's lover."

"You're going mad, Giorgia."

"He was an actor."

"Who?"

"The A. I've spoken to you about."

"And what about this guy?"

I tell him to fuck off, and I go back into the room. Dazi is putting on his coat. "Here you are," he says, handing me the note pad. "Too bad I don't have a picture of her."

"Can you describe her to me?"

"She has a dreamy air. Tall, five-ten, quite beautiful…"

"Hair?"

"Dark blonde."

"Eyes?"

"Between gray and green."

"Thanks, I'll call you back."

He hesitates in the doorway, and I have the sensation that he's waiting for me to turn so he can check out my backside. "If you like, we could have dinner together to discuss my case more fully."

"That goes against my rules," I respond.

He smiles maliciously. "I imagined so."

"See you soon, Mr. Dazi."

"Goodbye, Doctor, and thanks."

"Hold off on thanking me. For all we know, at this moment your Angela could be in Bari or Los Angeles."

As soon as Dazi vanishes from my sight, I go into the bathroom and hit the cold water tap. I bend my head and see Spasimo peering at me.

"Fine looking man…"

I give him the stink eye.

"And the professor, the one at Tim's party?"

I raise my voice. "Lucio, by any chance, are you planning to marry me off?"

"Imagine that. With you, that would be a total waste of time."

"Yes, indeed."

"What's the name of this professor of performing arts?"

"Andrea Berti."

He puts on a detective's air: "Andrea. Interesting…"

After which, he turns around and struts away on the tips of his loafers like a movie star.

CHAPTER 6

I've often had the impression, since starting this work, that life — if you're going to live it in a dignified manner — ought to be one long silent scene. Gigiola is right: turn on the TV, and you only see people so flattened by soap opera talk that they are dying to make a spectacle of their own feelings or want to sell you something. There is all this anxiety to communicate, this bustle to make yourself visible, and the result is endless publicity — a long series of advertisements, of images that distance us from thinking about death during our leisure time and give us our daily dose of pornography. "Why did Alessandro Dazi come to my office?" I ask myself. Wouldn't it have been easier for him to make an appeal on a TV show like *Is There Any Mail for You?* Why should I have to dig up a girl whom he realizes that he's in love with twelve years later? But what is love anyway if people treat it like this?

I leave the agency talking to myself. I get into the car and call Tim right away.

"Are you up?" I shout into the cell phone so he can hear me.

"Well…"

"Get here right away."

"Yes, Mama."

"Listen, I wanted to know something about this professor of performing arts."

"You never trust anyone, do you?"

"What do you know about him?"

"He's a typical one."

"Be clear."

"He lives alone, lots of coeds find him attractive…"

"Where does he live?"

"How do I know? No, wait. One day I went by his place to pick up a book. He lives on Via Ferrarese, near the Piazza dell' Unità."

"The apartment number?"

"Oh, three or five. I don't remember."

"Nothing else?"

I hear him snicker. "He doesn't have a girlfriend. Are you interested in him?"

I blast my horn at a Ford Focus passing me on the right. "No, Tim. Is that all?"

"Let me think… Oh yeah, he has a cat. But you're not allergic, right?"

"Very witty."

I shift into reverse and speed off in the direction of Via Ferrarese. In front of number five on the other side of the street, I see a sign for "Dog and Cat." I park the Citroën between a Kia and a Matiz and enter the shop.

A sales girl in her twenties with a mass of red hair meets me in the doorway. "Would you like something?"

"I've just been given a cat. What food do you recommend?"

"Oh, we have different brands," she gushes, showing me an entire shelf of cans and cartons.

I look around: baskets, bedding, cages, collars, little balls, mice. The kingdom of the humanized animal. One day, dogs will recite Jacques Prévert.

"What breed?"

I'm distracted. "Who?"

"The kitten."

"Ah, no. He's a bastard."

"A mixed breed," she corrects me in a syrupy tone. "What color is he?"

I look at her hair. "Red."

"Wonderful…and what's his name?"

"Really…" I falter, "I haven't given him one yet — a name, I mean."

She's suspicious, maybe wondering if I'll drown the cat in the bath tub first thing this evening. "I recommend this cat food with tuna and also some kibbles…"

"Fine, please pack it up for me," I say, looking outside.

"Have you double-parked your car? At this hour, the traffic cops don't come by any longer…"

"No, I'm waiting for someone."

"Ah," she exclaims, putting a dozen cans inside a small bag.

I take a breath. "You don't by any chance know a certain Andrea Berti? He lives in that house." I point it out. "He also has a cat."

"Certainly, he's the one who teaches in the performing arts program," she says.

"Do you know him?"

"He's a client of mine…a nice looking man, huh?"

I extend my hand and give her a friendly smile. "I'm Giorgia."

"I'm Patrizia," she says, shaking my hand. "Patty."

"When does the professor usually return in the evening?"

She's well informed. "He always returns early, but I see him mainly when he comes here to buy food for his cat. One day he brought him here for me to see: an enormous striped cat, three-years old the first of April…"

Now she'll tell me his astrological sign.

I clear my throat with a cough. "I'll be honest with you, Patty. I'm a private investigator, and I'm allergic to cats."

She opens her mouth so wide that, for a moment, I make out her vocal cords.

"What can you tell me about him?"

"He's reserved, polite,…" she stammers. "All in all, a serious person. But what has he done? Has he gotten himself into trouble? Will you arrest him? Oh, I don't imagine you'll talk to me about it…"

"Well said."

"But?…"

"How much do I owe you, Patty?"

She gives me the bag with a trembling hand. "Twenty euros and fifty cents, the receipt is inside."

I pass her twenty-two euros. "Keep the change, and keep the cans, too."

I get back in the car but after half a mile, I park in front of Terry's Bar, squeezed between a news stand and a party favor store. I go inside and order a glass of white wine from the bartender, a curvaceous woman in her sixties with a bouffant hair style like Moira Orfei. "Plain or fizzy?" she asks me brusquely, hands on her hips.

"Plain."

The bar is empty. I sit at a corner table, glass in hand. I close my eyes, I drink, and then I order a second glass…

I have scattered images of my mother: of her sitting on the edge of the bed reading a book or arranging a bunch of flowers in a glass vase on top of the piano; the irregular beauty of her long, slender face; the dinners with friends of my father where she had the habit of turning to one person while staring at another; she whom my aunt defined as an "egotist"; she who, on certain winter evenings, used to take out the box for a game of Scrabble.

I recall one late autumn afternoon when she and I went shopping. We came home on foot in a sharp, freezing rain and a wind so strong it made us into hunchbacks, her black stockings splashed with mud, her shoulders shuddering lightly with laughter as I cried out to her: "Mama, I can't keep up, your legs are too long."

Terry, the bartender, lowers the metal awning of the bar and takes a seat at my table with a large, half-full bottle of wine.

As often happens when I'm drunk, I offer up the high points of my life to the first pair of willing ears.

"Who hasn't thought of killing herself at least once? You know how it is, working in a bar, I've heard so many stories. You really don't expect that some people, with their smiles, their composure, could do such a thing…"

Then she smacks a hand, with blood-red nails, on top of the little table. "Twenty years with an alcoholic! Twenty years! If a kid comes into the bar now and rolls a joint, I take him straight to the police!"

"Your husband?"

"My ex-husband. If you only knew what I went through…"

Then she starts to tell me everything: infidelities, binges, debts, quarrels. But my head is somewhere else — that day at the seaside so many years ago, when a twelve-year-old boy from Varese was dragged dead onto the beach, green all over, with a life guard giving him mouth to mouth, right in front of his mother, waiting on the shore for him with a beach towel in her hands.

"It was there I learned the big difference between a whirlpool that sucks you down and a car that smashes against a gate…"

Maybe I spoke too loud.

Terry, unsure whether to call the emergency phone line or simply invite me to leave the bar, grabs the bottle of wine, raises up the awning, and lets in another customer.

I take out the notebook from my purse. "Nervous breakdown. G. makes me eat. He cleans up the bathroom three times a week. I push my own buttons…" (I hear you, Ada. Letters, words that I listen to like a record. It's the sound of your pain. But I don't forgive you, I don't forgive either one of you two.)

I leave the bar, swaying from side to side up to the car. On the cell phone there's a missed call from Gaia, so I head for Via Saragozza, hoping I'm not stopped on the way by a cop for the balloon test.

One honk of the horn and Gaia comes down, opens the electric gate, and dives into my car.

"Your mother?" I ask.

"She's out for dinner. Guess with whom…"

"I'm sorry, but sooner or later I have to speak to your father."

"I know. He returns from Lugano in a week."

"You haven't said anything to him?"

She stares in front of her. "I'm not a spy."

I open a packet of Kleenex, take one, and blow my nose.

"Do you have a cigarette?" she asks. "I should tell you something."

I hand her a Camel, and on the third try, my almost empty Bic lighter spits out a tiny flame. "What is it?"

She picks at a nail. "Last night Tim called me."

I'm surprised.

"He wanted to invite me to the Link for a beer."

"Did you go?"

She twists her lips. "Yes."

"So?"

"A friend of his was also there."

"Viola?"

"She's very pretty, right?"

"You're also pretty."

She shakes her head and sucks on the cigarette like a newborn at the nipple.

"He told me he feels out of place…that he and Fede belong to a parallel society…"

(I think of that brain-dead Fede, Tim's scrawny and pimply soul-mate, who sweats constantly and never bathes.)

"Then he talked to me about India, where he went last year. He doesn't know anyone, but he wants to go back there…"

I've had enough. "Gaia," I say, tossing the Kleenex out the window, "better for you to know one thing right away. When Tim smokes, he says a lot of shit to make himself look good to the girls. He's never been to India, and not to Australia either, in case he told you that, too."

A maid is calling Adam, the Comolli family boxer, in a loud voice.

Gaia looks outside. "I believe everything," she says sadly. "He asked me if I was in Genoa at the time of the G8 meeting protests, and I told him no. I think I've disillusioned him."

She slips out of the car and walks toward the gate. The dog comes up to her and licks her hand.

I park the car outside the house. I get out. As I insert the key in the glass-pane door, I glimpse a shadow limping near me. In the faint light of the door-bell frame, I recognize Giordano Lattice.

"I've been waiting an hour for you," he tells me. "I've also tried you on your cell phone."

"I'm very tired… What do you want?"

He turns sarcastic. "You could give me your condolences, I suppose."

"Have you come here to tell me that you're suffering?"

He stifles a laugh. "I'm not the type to talk about these things in public."

"Have you been drinking, Lattice?"

"No, I'm sober. Disgustingly sober, Ms. Cantini, unlike you."

He leans his weight against the wall, bending his knee slightly. "What have you told the police?"

"Listen," I say, searching in my purse for cigarettes and a lighter, "you shouldn't be here."

"Yes, I know. I'm always in the wrong place. For example, I wasn't at my wife's house when I should have been there."

"So, what do you want? Have you finally come to pay me?"

He stares at me. "I'm certain that the person who killed her is in that photo."

"The photos are with the police. It's up to them now, Lattice. Or are you thinking about playing Charles Bronson in this situation?"

"I've spent all this time seeing her in my head while she fucks Tizio and Caio... You have no idea what torture it is to imagine things like this."

He snatches off his wool beret. My eyes open wide at the sight of his hair, tinted the ridiculous yellow of polenta. How long has he been sporting this look?

"I've also thought about ending my life, but I'm Catholic."

(Great excuse.)

"I loved her." He looks at me. "Oh, you can't understand."

I'd like to ask him why I can't understand, but my head is spinning, and I can't wait for him to leave me in peace.

"Destiny did not take her life, Ms. Cantini, nor did illness. A man did, who screwed her and then..."

He bursts into tears like a child.

"Lattice," I say, touching his shoulder, "what can I do for you? Tell me. Do you have a good lawyer?"

He shrugs his shoulders and walks off into the darkness, sobbing.

I go into the house, shake off Lattice and his troubles, and throw myself on the bed.

Ada's letters have changed location: they cover the quilted bedspread and sleep with me.

I wonder if she was expecting a baby and, if so, who was the father: Giulio or A.?

I wonder why her friend Anna is never mentioned in these letters and how I can track her down, not having in my possession either a last name or any clue that will lead to her.

In the morning I could pester Aldo Cinelli and Giulio Manfredini, but I have the feeling they know as much as I do. I know I'll get nothing out of my father.

My father.

He and I — two survivors who drink to forget.

And to forget, they say, is a defeat. Or is Gigiola right: drinking is the other face of clarity.

I was nine when I went to find Grandmother Lina at the hospital. She was in bed: skeletal, almost bald, unrecognizable. She tried to touch me and I moved away. "I'm hideous, aren't I?" she said, hiding her face in her yellow, wrinkled hands. I placed a pair of uncertain fingers on the sheet: an unsuccessful gesture. There was no hope, the doctors said, and the only thing Grandmother Lina wanted was to die at home. My mother was full of egotistical hope for a miracle: "At St. Ursula's Hospital they can cure her, they can take care of her…" In a few words, save her. Hope is an instinct, she told us. And medicine is not an exact science.

Grandmother was more dead than alive. Everyone realized it, including me, a small child. She died the day after my visit, in that anonymous hospital room, alone like a dog. Afterwards, mama tortured herself with remorse. "I should have carried her back home!" she cried. "Why did I leave her there? She should have died in her own bed, peacefully."

The sense of guilt.

The most modern illness there is. Just takes a crumb of ego to wallow in it. My father and I have been mired in that shit (it's true, isn't it?) for a lifetime.

"Enjoy with moderation, suffer with dignity," the classics say. What did I study at school? What did they tell me at catechism? Pain is like guilt. Do you suffer? That means you've strayed from God. Go fuck yourself. Pain is innocent, pain is part of life.

I speak out loud — to whom, I don't know. Did you know there are catholic doctors who won't give morphine to terminally ill patients because they say pain is expiation, that it purifies you?

Yes, yes, you're right, I've been drinking. But what does that matter? Really, what does that matter? Even insects get stoned. Bees travel for miles to suck nectar from certain flowers that make them drunk! There has never existed a culture on earth that hasn't had the need to get stoned…both primitive and religious people. You know what I say? Sober folks love the truth; drunkards don't. And I'm up to my ass in guilt and truth!

I go to sleep.

CHAPTER 7

Do I see the others? Or are they all shadows? Where is the real time? Who has hidden it from me?

I wake up with a jolt, take a quick shower, get dressed, and leave the house. My second-floor neighbor blocks me in front of the elevator and tells me about the Reggiani's poodle on the third floor, how he barked all night and kept her awake. I visualize mentally the little dog, dirty-white and curly-haired, whom the sixteen-year-old son of Mrs. Reggiani has nicknamed Van Damme. "A name more suitable for a pit bull," I told Mrs. Reggiani some time ago, but she didn't understand my remark. She didn't know who Van Damme was.

My neighbor informs me that they'll be hearing from her at the next condo meeting. She loves animals, but there's a limit to everything: they should muzzle that dog, give him a sedative, strong enough to make him stop barking. I tell her she's right, even though I slept soundly and never heard Van Damme. At that moment, from the glass-paned door, I see a scooter arrive at the entrance way.

Tim gets off the seat and removes his helmet; he comes striding toward me, the elastic band of his boxers sticking out from his jeans. He tells me he has time for a coffee, then he'll go back home to study.

I scan him from head to foot. "Impressive bags under your eyes! Spend the night on PlayStation?"

I'm obviously teasing him.

"Want to smoke?" he asks me, glancing at the joint in his hand.

"It's eleven in the morning, Tim."

"Yeah, I know, it's still dawn."

I decide to start the day with a few tokes of weed.

I call Bruni on my cell phone in the car. I ask him if there's any news on the Verze case, but I keep to myself the encounter with Lattice outside my house last night. Bruni tells me they're questioning both the wife's and the husband's close friends.

"Do you know what Lattice does for a living?" he asks me.

"Sure, he has a club."

"The Cocorito. A kind of night club with strippers, lap dancers, private parties. His poker friends, go figure, all work at the Cocorito."

"Ah."

"Has he tried to contact you?"

"No," I lie.

"He did a few years in prison for theft and receipt of stolen goods. Did you know that?"

I don't answer.

"We've been putting the screws to him for eighteen hours... sooner or later he'll snap."

"And if he didn't do it?"

"What, are you playing Nancy Drew now?"

We laugh.

"No, Bruni," and I'm being sincere. "I have some personal problems at the moment. I've already told you about Lattice, and I haven't seen any sign of him."

"It's up to the judge to decide if he's going to be held in custody. But for now he's a free man, Giorgia." I hear him sigh. "All in all, what's your impression of him?"

"Well...he's not a scary guy. Look...I just don't see him strangling somebody with his own hands."

"The world is full of killers who aren't scary. Close neighbors, fathers with families...all people you'd never suspect."

I reflect out loud. "Is it so hard to deal with a divorce? I mean, at the cost of murdering someone?"

"Don't you read the papers? Every day, somewhere, there's a man who wipes out an entire family."

"Yes, and at the end he can't endure the guilt and kills himself. Meanwhile Lattice is alive and well."

"Giorgia, let's not joke around. We constantly interrogate men and women who only care about one thing: their domination of other people. They live for years with the same person. They sleep together and wake up together. Then, out of the blue, that person becomes their worst enemy."

(I'd like to tell him that I know all about it. I listen to lots of people like this.) "The fact remains, Lattice has an alibi."

"Despite that, he also has an excellent motive."

I hear the voice of someone calling him. Bruni excuses himself. "I have to go. See you soon."

At six minutes past noon, I enter Enzo's bar where Lucia Tolomelli stands waiting for me at the counter with the expression of someone who already understands everything. If she needed a confirmation, my eyes speak clearly.

I invite her to sit at a corner table and order a coffee for her and a Campari for me. Now the most difficult thing is to take these damned photos from the envelope and place them in her lap.

Lucia removes the plastic covering and examines them one by one, careful not to smudge them as she spreads them out on the dirty table top. She smiles bitterly: "I was right."

I remain silent, neutral as a plant, sipping my Campari.

"I have two children. Do you have children?"

"No." I avoid adding "fortunately."

"What should I do? Leave him or continue this farce?"

I look at the pictures of billiard tournaments hanging on the walls.

"What infuriates me most," she adds with a tension-racked voice, "is that, among all the women out there, he set his eyes on my cousin."

I avoid her glance. "These things often happen in families."

Lucia starts to sob. I move my chair to shield her from indiscreet eyes and speak the typical nonsense you say in situations like this: that grief is liberating, that she's just received a blow, that (you never know) Alfio might come to his senses, that she might be the one to meet someone else.

She shakes her head fiercely. Something drips from her nostrils.

I lift up the untasted cup of coffee and hand her the little paper napkin from the saucer underneath. She thanks me and blows her nose loudly, then opens her purse and takes out her wallet. I get up. Nothing more to say.

Sentiments — to hell with them. Hugging herself in her burgundy coat, she raises her head and grabs at a shred of self-control. "Your money," she says. "Do you prefer a check?"

"Don't worry about it."

She smiles and nods at my red eye. "You should see a specialist."

I smile back. I go to the cashier, pay for the Campari and coffee, and wait for her to leave.

I eat lunch at Enzo's bar: a prosciutto sandwich and a medium Pepsi. Sitting on a stool, I leaf through the paper until I get to the horoscope page. Every line makes me mutter: "bullshit." Then I lift my eyes and see the identical twin of Alvaro Zincati enter the bar: the same smile, same hair style... It's not him, though. I breathe a sigh of relief.

Our affair lasted six months. Alvaro Zincati would call me at night and drop by for sex, really good sex. We had in common a few books we read in our youth, some seventies rock groups, and tummy fat. We both liked to talk about the past. He used to say: "I only drink when I'm thirsty." (More or less the same thing I say to my father with an air of superiority.) When he stopped calling, he stopped, and that was it. He gave no explanations, and there were no explanations to give. He seemed to take his wife and kids for granted whenever he spoke about them, as if they'd always be there, framed in a ten-by-twelve color photo, with dog and bungalow in the background, on the desk of his law office. He cut loose with me, acted like a little boy, told me stories from his childhood, and blurted out all kinds of stuff: "What do you think of a weekend in Vienna or Paris?" We never went to Vienna or Paris, never went to a restaurant, never left my house a single time. I can see him naked in bed, with his hard, muscular legs covered in blonde hair, a wide smile, and the flaring nostrils of someone who nuzzles and sniffs you like some primordial creature.

Then, one night, he didn't show up, and he never looked for me again.

If I were someone who believes that one letter would do the job, I would have written him. But in situations like this letters are stupid things you soon regret. You pour yourself out writing them, and you get nothing in return. No lover that leaves you wants to answer your letter. It's the same for the telephone. What's the point of phoning someone who's decided to make himself scarce? Sure, I spent a few weeks waiting for the phone to ring. My house had become a waiting room. I don't believe people who claim they've never waited for any one. We all wait. We're always waiting. For one thing or another.

My eyes light on the sign for Taurus (Alvaro was born on May 16). *Advice for the day: "Spend the evening with your family. Ultimately, you'll forget about your cares."* I'm certain he has another lover, and the thought of it makes me smile. I shut the paper.

The bar is full of people who are eating lunch standing up before going back to the office, to their goldfish bowls and piles of paper on metal desks. There's every type here: the usual seat warmers, the executives in their designer clothes, guys peddling sunglasses and lighters, people with flabby, worn-out faces who greet each other with indifference, dusty old folks reading the paper, girls controlling their nerves as if they are tottering on high heels. Tired laughter comes at me from every corner. I get up and leave.

At 4:08 in the afternoon, I'm in the orthodontist office of Alvise Lumini. He opens the door dressed in a white unbuttoned shirt, which tells me that he is rushed for time and is expecting a patient any moment. He welcomes me into a waiting room with four chairs, a wooden bench, completely bare walls, and a table in the center full of old magazines. He masks his anxiety with forced cheerfulness, sitting on the bench where he takes up almost all the space, but he can't stay still. In fact, he gets up and opens the window to let in a little light.

"I've made some inquiries and…I have to admit that, yes, Serena, your Serena…"

He interrupts me, "You've met her?"

"Just now."

He gets excited. "Don't you find her incredibly beautiful? Isn't she the most beautiful woman you've ever seen?"

"Yes, she's very beautiful," I reassure him.

"I just knew it. I'm an idiot. I should never have doubted her."

I open my mouth to talk, but it's not easy to tell the truth to someone who doesn't want to hear it. "Signor Lumini, Serena has some flaws."

He slaps his large hands on his knees. "And who doesn't?" (He's correct.) "She used to sell herself."

"True, in the beginning she didn't work at the dressmaker's shop. She sold clothes at home, but for a much lower price…"

I don't flinch. "She's an ex-prostitute."

"Certainly, certainly…"

Silence falls.

When he starts talking again, his voice is strange. "We've already made up the invitation list. Around thirty people — a nice number. We've reserved a church and a restaurant in Pianoro. Serena has chosen the wedding favors herself, and I'm taking care of the guests. For wedding presents, we're expecting a dishwasher and a trip to Tenerife. I'd like at least three children. I come from a big family, you know."

I look at him. His face is red and warm. He clinches his hand in a fist. He doesn't want to know about my version of the facts. Every version is unfaithful, even if there are some things that don't allow room for interpretation, and Serena's past is one of these. Perhaps Alvise is capable of accepting that no one is perfect. Perhaps he only gets pleasure out of something that can do serious harm to his health. Perhaps Serena makes him weep with joy, and this is the only thing that matters. Perhaps he's thinking, as he looks out the window at a bird pecking a branch, that it was a mistake to come to me. Perhaps he's decided to disregard the judgmental attitude and moral code of his family from Belluno. Perhaps he wants to pull the bed sheet up to his chin the way children do when they're scared. Perhaps I've instilled a doubt in him that will never go away. Perhaps everything true like this ends up being false. The doorbell rings. His patient has arrived. Alvise Lumini gets up from the bench. "I've already put the money in your account."

We shake hands.

At six in the afternoon, I go into a bar downtown and sit in front of a gin bitter. I've parked far away because, at this hour, with all the cars, trucks, bikes, scooters, vans, taxis, skateboards, et cetera, the traffic snarls more from aggression than from smog.

A short, blonde waitress darts between the tables, picking up empty glasses and setting down full ones, with the sullen look of someone who has to work until dawn for nickels and dimes. The neon lights illuminate the teeth of the customers: the artificial whiteness of people who go to the dentist for cosmetic treatment. I reach for my glass with one arm and with the other I hug my belly, as though caressing my digestive track will ease some of my bad eating habits.

I watch a man (he's loosened his tie) courting with desperate cynicism a girl in a suit, undoubtedly a young assistant in his office. They drink their aperitifs and fill their mouths with appetizers. I see them undulate, lethargic and relaxed, erasing with liquor the memory of the recent work day. People go to the bar searching for other people, but almost never find them. Alcohol separates more than it unites. It's a resistant and divisive glass wall.

I press the icy drink to my cheek to keep me awake, and I realize that no one here wants to stop being young. At the age of twenty-two, I held my first glass, and then and there all my lessons in self-discipline vanished. At eighteen, I had heard Ada say that heroin was a medicinal drug. That's what her addict friends told her, the ones who injected it and then collapsed in her arms as though she were the Red Cross. Cocaine came next. She snorted it at the Pineta Disco in Milano Marittima, where my sister went dancing every Saturday night...

If anyone ever criticized my way of dressing, it was Ada. On my side of the armoire: loose-fitting jeans, tennis shoes, and large sweatshirts. On her side: skirts and tops (high-neck, theatrically black) and outfits that revealed her personality and originality. The time she tried to put make-up on me, I rushed to the bathroom to wash my face. I was convinced that femininity didn't have to be expressed through greasepaint and lipstick. Ada used to tell me that I'd never find someone because men were put off by my mug. These are just stupid stereotypes, I told her, but she was right.

Ada didn't have female friends, that is, not true friends. She fascinated all the girls because she was magnetic and a bit of a show off, but the boys liked her, and this made her dangerous. My sister reminded me of Lais, the ancient Greek courtesan, who was stoned to death (I think) in the temple of Aphrodite by women jealous of her beauty. It was touching, sometimes, to see her contort her perfect features into cabaret grimaces so that she could seem trusting and kind. It didn't work. Her girlfriends were only passing presences in our house. They changed all the time. They didn't last more than a few months.

I have the round brown eyes of my father. Ada's eyes were narrow and gray like mama's. I thought Ada's eyes were much more beautiful than mine, and I told her that they were just like Charlotte Rampling's.

"Do you want eyes like Claudia Cardinale's?" she replied.

"Do you think my eyes are like hers?" I asked.

"No, yours are more beautiful."

Naturally, I didn't believe her, but I also thought when people say that a friend is like a sister, what they really mean is that she tells you lies just like these.

For a while, Ada used to bring home one of her classmates, a certain Michela, shy and skinny. Michela liked a tall, blond, blue-eyed boy (the classic type), who played basketball. One

October afternoon at the Artists Bar, he told Ada he liked her, that is, he gave her a chain with a red heart made of glass. She left the bar. He followed her, pressed her against a column, and started to kiss her. I saw the scene unfold through the front window of the bar, holding a cup of cappuccino, with a petrified Michela sitting beside me, looking in the same direction. When the boy left on his blue Vespa, Ada returned to the bar, came up to her friend, took her hand, and wrapped the chain around the girl's fingers like a rosary. The next day, the boy went to pick up my sister at her piano lesson, and she suggested that he go out with Michela. He never did. I never saw Michela in our house again.

I leave the bar and take a long walk. I pass in front of a tanning salon, formerly a book store. After a few yards, I stop in front of a shoe display, recalling how this used to be a record store, only a year ago.

CHAPTER 8

Why didn't I become a lawyer? That's the question I ask myself, sitting on the edge of the tub, wrapped in a towel, while I count the drops that fall from my soaked hair and form a puddle on the linoleum floor. I get up. I raise the organza curtain and see the well-lit windows of the building in front: families that sit at the table and watch the TV news. I know why I didn't become a lawyer: because the day I was supposed to defend my thesis I was with my father in a funeral store to select a coffin.

I leave the bathroom and stretch out on the bed.

Once again, the letters are in the shoe box on the rug. If I hang over the side of the bed, I see them.

January 27, 1986

I've been waiting over an hour for A. in front of the Trilussa monument in Trastevere. Do you know the movie Querelle*? Jeanne Moreau says to Querelle: "Finally. Why did you make me wait so long? Do you want to hurt me? Do you want to destroy me? My desire for you is so intense, so deep...." And he: "What are you talking about? What are you crying about? Why have you longed for me? And who is it that you're longing for...do you want to know?"*

I saw my mother's lover only once, in church, the day of her funeral. He was a stocky man, about five-foot seven, with black, deep-set eyes and the smooth cheeks of a baby. He stood in front of the entrance to the church, wearing a dark coat and staring at the ground. I watched Ada for a long while with a sad smile. At a certain point during the Mass, I turned to look for him, but he wasn't there anymore.

I never saw him again, and I don't know how long his affair with my mother lasted, but it was clear that not even he managed to make her happy.

My mother.

She didn't laugh very often, but when she did, she never stopped. "Ilaria, stop it," my father would say. They never quarreled, but they weren't affectionate either. I assumed they loved each other secretly. Ada had told me that opposites attract.

Mama had her visions, her spaces for extra-marital thrills, and her pills. I still see the quick movement of her hand to her mouth. She downed the pills without drinking anything; she swallowed them with her eyes closed, and she was only tranquil like this — with her mind shut down.

"Mama was too sensitive," Ada said with a throaty voice and gleaming eyes, a few months after the funeral.

"Oh, the sensitive ones," my aunt burst out. "Always ready to yell with pain as soon as someone steps on their foot but oblivious when they tread on someone else's foot."

I believe they started insulting each other while my father, on the telephone with someone, didn't bother to listen. My sister threw me looks of cold astonishment: "Why don't you intervene? Why don't you say something?" she seemed to ask me.

One evening, returning home from my English lesson, I found my father in the kitchen, in the dark, sitting near the French door that opened onto the garden. It hit me hard to see him so distraught, so vulnerable — he who was always as tough as an oak. Those were long nights for the three of us. We looked like mismatched chairs spread around the table with its plastic flower tablecloth. At dinner, he complained about pains in his side owing to the change in the seasons, but later, when he was alone (and we in our bedroom upstairs), he took out his bottle of Anisette from the cabinet.

The phone wakes me at noon. I open my eyes in the dark and run to the living room before the message machine starts up. Alessandro Dazi, the voice-over actor, wishes me good morning.

I explain to him curtly that I've taken a day off. He apologizes and asks me if he can invite me to breakfast. I decline the offer, but I inform him that I'll be going to Rome tomorrow to do some research on Angela, "the only woman he's ever loved in his life."

In the afternoon I book a round-trip ticket. Then I shave my legs and underarms using a cream whose expiration date had passed, as I watch a TV movie about a woman who accuses her father of sexual abuse that began when she was a baby. At seven in the evening, I receive an unexpected phone call. Andrea Berti tells me that he got my number from Tim. Humming and hawing, he admits the reason for his call: Would I like to have dinner with him somewhere, or do I have another engagement? My silence goes on for an embarrassing length, and he's forced to repeat his proposal.

"Why not?" I say at the end.

An hour later, I park the Citroën on Via D'Azeglio and walk all the way down Via Solferino under a pouring rain. I'm almost at the Trattoria Trebbi when I hear a voice right behind me: "Quo vadis, baby?" I turn around, and Andrea Berti smiles at me from a few feet away.

We enter the warmth of the place and hang up our soaked jackets. In a corner, a chalkboard with the specialty of the day. I immediately light up a Camel and order a carafe of red wine from the fat waitress.

I'm afraid I don't have topics to talk about, so for several minutes I ask him about Tim and how things are going in the department. When the pumpkin tortellini arrives, I feel his leg touch mine. I move aside and start to eat.

A couple comes in and sits at the table next to us.

"Why do you look at everybody in that way?" the professor asks me.

"Sorry, in what way?"

He smiles. "I understand. All potential enemies."

"Why aren't you with a woman?"

"You're very direct."

I nod as I eat.

"Things happen in a person's life…"

"I understand. She dumped you for your best friend."

He has a low pleasant laugh. "It's not so simple."

"Then explain it to me."

"Sorry, but I don't feel like it."

I shrug my shoulders. "I unmask people, and everyone likes their disguises."

"Maybe you let your work into your life too much."

I wipe my mouth with the napkin. "Perhaps."

For the second course, Andrea Berti chooses a plate of mixed greens, and I order a green-pepper filet of beef.

"You don't strike me as a shy type," I say, looking straight at him.

"How do I strike you?"

"As an intellectual, who's going to deliver me an essay on his sense of irony and his critical approach."

He slaps his knee with laughter, as if I'd said something witty.

"You know," I tell him, "I don't like today's forty-something men…"

"Why not?"

"They seem to me like adolescents trapped inside aging bodies."

"Too bad," he says jokingly, "I only go out with women my own age."

I blow smoke in his direction, and he rubs his eyes.

I like it when he takes me suddenly without foreplay. My body feels alive then and my head detached from the rest. It's like dancing the tango…

"What are you thinking about?"

"Sorry, I'm distracted. Nothing really."

Stupid phrases from Ada's letters churn in my head, while I feel a flow of energy pass from me to him.

"What kind of relationship are you interested in?" he asks me randomly.

"None."

"Whose fault is that?"

"Not many men are good at it."

"At doing what?"

"Falling in love with me."

He laughs ambiguously. "Is this a challenge?"

"Yeah, right, I've never learned how to flirt. Do you want dessert?"

When we leave the trattoria, Andrea Berti asks me for a ride to his house. I pretend I don't know the neighborhood where he lives, and I make him give me the necessary directions. I stop the car in front of number five, and he asks me if I want to come up for a cup of tea or an after-dinner drink. I accept and follow him up two flights of stairs. He takes a while to find his keys (maybe he's nervous). Finally, we go inside, and he turns on the hallway light. I see myself reflected in a mirror on the wall, blowing smoke from my Camel as if it were oxygen. Andrea Berti takes my cigarette and puts it out in a flower pot. We kiss.

As he guides me along, I glimpse cinema books stacked on top of each other in his library, a pair of boxer shorts and Adidas sneakers on the floor, dark curtains on the windows, nutritional supplements on the kitchen table, and a huge cat with an unfathomable expression curled up on top of a cabinet full of drawers. Andrea opens the frosted-glass door to the bedroom without removing his tongue from my mouth.

We strip.

I hear his breathless words, I feel his body taught with urgent desire, I smell the soap from his underarms. As he thrusts, gropes, licks, plunges, caresses, I turn ten again, and everything is all right. My mother is talking on the phone with her friend Teresa, my sister is in front of the mirror reciting "The Blind Woman" by Rilke, and my father won't return home for another hour. It just takes a splash of cold water on my face in the bathroom for me to come back to earth. Andrea

Berti is asleep, and I wander around his apartment on tiptoe. I can't restrain myself; I look for addresses, old pictures, papers in drawers, and the cat doesn't spring at me — a harmless creature. With a sense of relief, I find nothing important. I put on my clothes and leave the apartment.

At home, I grab Ada's box of letters and hide it under the usual pile of tops in the usual armoire.

CHAPTER 9

I'm sitting in the smoking car of this Eurostar train, with circles under my eyes from four hours of sleep, thinking about the attention I've received from the hands of Andrea Berti.

My cell phone rings, and after three "hellos" I finally make out the voice of Alessandro Dazi whining about something I don't understand. I calmly wait for a sensible phrase to emerge from his mouth and discover that Angela De Santis, his very own Angela, died six years ago in an accident. He's just learned this from an old mutual friend, who called him after hearing from other people that Alessandro was looking for her. End of investigation — that's all I'm able to think about.

"I'll never find another woman like her," he laments. "Certain events happen only once in a lifetime…"

I pretend to play along with an "Oh, I understand." This tragic event, Dazi says, confirms the fact that she was the woman of his life and that destiny wanted to punish him. He apologizes for making me leave town, and he can't wait to see me again so he can pay me my fee.

I get off the train and go straight to check out the schedule for departures to Bologna, intending to take the first one. Then, impulsively, I leave the station, climb into a taxi and tell the driver, "Piazza della Malva."

In front of number six, I lean my weight against a Ritmo with flat tires and three cats asleep on its rusty hood. I light a Camel and look at the second-floor window.

I've never seen this mini-apartment, and I have no idea who lives here now, but as I lift my eyes toward the only window that overlooks the piazza, I realize that there, behind those white curtains, my sister killed herself.

It's like being in front of her tomb, and I can't stand it that everything around here is so calm and tranquil, that people come and go, walk their dogs, buy papers at the newsstands, take their breakfast at the same bar where she probably spent days waiting for some audition. I imagine the long empty pauses in front of the telephone, the fear of hearing that they've taken another actress for that role or that she should call back in a week's time — a week that becomes a month, a month that becomes a season, and then there's the daughter of the set designer or the girl next in line for promotion or the one that's screwing the director or the producer. In short, there's always someone ahead of her.

The sky is darkening. Piazza della Malva is behind me. I look at this city of cats and ruins from the taxi window, the lamp lights reflecting on the Tiber, the ancient and the modern jumbled together; I recall that remark of Plato to an older woman jealous of a young girl: "I prefer your wrinkles to some youngster's bonfire." Rome. Here's the city my sister loved. The city where, according to her, important things happened and where her life would start over. I hear the driver say something about the time, and I feel deeply languid and weary. My eyelids lower.

My sister enters the room with eyes red from chlorine, throws her gym bag on the floor, removes her soaking wet swimsuit and bath towel and spreads them out on the radiator. She combs her hair and puts on lipstick in front of the old mirror. I lean out the window and see a boy lounging against the car door of a broken down Maggiolone. "Who's that guy waiting for you down there?" She shrugs her shoulders, leaves the room, and runs to the street. I go to the window and see her. She walks in front of the car's headlights and gives the boy a dazzling smile. "Ada!" I shout. "Ada! If you don't come home by five, Papa…"

The driver stops. Two times, I ask him what the trip costs. He repeats the sum with strained politeness.

Back in Bologna, I retrieve my Citroën from the station parking lot and drive home. I squeeze the car between a Megane and a Ka, get out, and as I head for the glass-paned door, I hear noises. I turn around, look to the right and the left No one. The darkness is thick. The wind shakes the branches of the sweet gum trees that line my little street.

At home I walk on bare feet and mark my passage by running my finger across dust-coated furniture, books, and photo albums. Then I collapse on the sofa, dead tired, with the weary eyes of someone who has seen enough for one day.

The answering machine shows that Andrea Berti hasn't called. Should he have? After all, what are a few hours of intimate words, kisses, and embraces? "It's dangerous to lean out": they put this warning on trains. If he were to lean towards me, he'd discover things he wouldn't like. That's for certain. I open a can of beer. What do I know about Andrea Berti? Practically nothing. But this is how it works, right? You live through an experience and then you think about it. You set your imagination in motion. You alter reality, and then you can't remember anymore how something actually happened.

I fall asleep at once.

The next day I spend the morning trying to get in touch with Guido Comolli, the engineer. Then I have lunch with Tim in a self-service place on Via Righi. His stomach looks hollow under his red sweatshirt. His Levi underwear sticks out from his sagging jeans.

Incredible but true, he has Baudelaire's *Flowers of Evil* in the pocket of his jacket. So I ask myself if Gaia had a hand in this and if these two are seeing each other. When I glance at the book, Tim says, "Shit, poetry is important."

I don't comment on the fact that he's blushing. "Sorry, I thought you only read Brizzi."

I watch him take out a dung-like piece of hashish, papers, and a cigarette, and I drag him away from the self-service before somebody else kicks him out.

As we walk along Via Indipendenza, he tells me that he stayed up late last night with Fede at the Irish Pub. They smoked ten joints, drank seven pints of beer, played guitar and bass at Picchio's house...

"Gaia?" I ask.

He jerks his head at me. "Did she tell you something?"

Now I have proof: they're seeing each other.

"Berti called," Spasimo informs me as soon as I enter the office. He's holding a small paper cup of coffee. "Do you want it? I haven't put sugar in it."

"No thanks." I drop down on the sofa. "I'll never figure this out..."

He sits back down at the computer. "Why don't you call him back?"

"Who?"

"You know very well who I'm talking about."

I twist my hair with one hand. "I'm referring to my sister."

"Ah," he sighs.

I change the subject. "What are you working on?"

"I'm checking the anti-virus programs and updating software to define the business operation of...but what am I talking to you for? This doesn't mean anything to you."

I place my hands on my knees and get up from the sofa. "You're right." In the doorway, I turn and say, "For the past few days, I feel like I'm being followed."

His face grows dark. "You're kidding."

"I'm not. It's only a feeling."

"Have you spoken to Bruni about it?"

"Just the usual ghosts, Lucio. Or else I'm going insane."

I'm too tired and impatient to work, so I fool around on the PC, drop by the bar, skim through old paperwork, but above all annoy Lucio the entire afternoon.

I have an appointment at eight with Mel — he just returned from a trade show in Madrid — at the Café de Paris for an after dinner drink.

I'm glad to see someone who's been my friend since I was a kid and who knows so much about me. The first time he heard me play the drums he asked me why I was so angry at the world.

Mel knew Ada and liked her. "The whole time you're talking to her, she's looking somewhere else," he told me one day.

"She's just a bit spacey and distracted," I came to her defense.

"I know women," said Mel, "and when a woman looks at something that only she can see, it makes a man feel like a moron."

Mel knew about my mother. I had talked about her at length during one of those sunrise sessions with beer-and-chips, when we left the rehearsal hall, soaked in sweat, and filed into a tavern on Via Fondazza. His mother died when he was ten years old, and the night before her death she had started making desserts.

"She had the feeling she'd be going away that night," he told me.

The time he spoke to me about it, I asked myself why I didn't have a mother like Mel's — one who makes desserts for her kids and goes away because fate has reserved a damn tumor for her.

Mel gives me a smack on the shoulder and orders a gin bitter. "Two," I say to the bartender with the Rasta hairstyle and the eyebrow piercing.

"I got to know a girl from Monaco," he confides in me. "I'm meeting her tonight. She's twenty-two, and I already imagine the moment in which she'll chew me up and spit out the pieces. From someone who listens to the New Radicals, what can you expect?"

"Some people at twenty are a lot smarter than us," I tell him.
"Do you know that film, *The Ambiguous Nature of Love?*"
I shake my head.

"At a certain point the man says something like: "I've never met anyone born after 1965 who wasn't half baked. It's the fault of the microwave oven.""

We laugh and clink our glasses. "To your new affair, Mel," I say without irony. "May it last longer than a month."

He takes a long sip of his gin bitter. "May it last as long as it needs to."

Half an hour later, I drive toward Andrea Berti's apartment with a sack full of Chinese food. The only parking place I find is in front of the Dog & Cat store, so I rush to slip inside the apartment before Patty, the sales clerk, is aware of my presence.

Andrea is bare-chested, wearing a pair of faded jeans and reading glasses that dangle from a little cord. "You don't call. You just show up."

"Are you hungry?" I ask. He takes the sack from me and puts it on the kitchen table. He looks down, tapping his foot on the terracotta floor. When he raises his eyes, I feel as if I were swimming butterfly in a pool. "Later," he says.

We make love two times, with our flaws exposed like weaknesses that we exchange with each other: my tits at war with the force of gravity, his soft (lazy intellectual) belly. He starts to play with my pubic hair like a child in a field hunting four-leaf clovers; I bend tenderly to kiss his flaccid, wet prick. We look at each other by lamp light, stretched out on the dreamy blue-and-green comforter. I smoke, and he sips from a bottle of Black & White whiskey.

Later, while we devour chicken curry on the bed, I muster my courage: "I used to have a sister. They say she killed herself."

I see his jaw muscle twitch: "They say?"

"Do you believe in God?"

He shakes his head as he chews.

"It's strange how the absence of people you love can make you believe in a life after this…"

He gets up, crushes the plastic containers, and throws them in the trash. "There's no life after this, Giorgia. The only thing we don't know is our expiration date."

I rest my weight against the cushioned head board. "A fine sentence, professor, a bit like *Blade Runner*. I'll write it down in my journal as soon as I go home."

He's disappointed. "You're not sleeping here?"

"I'm not used to sleeping with someone."

He inserts *When* by Vincent Gallo in the CD player. "How many people have you pushed into that dark corner?"

I force myself to laugh. "But what do you mean?"

I watch him leave the room and head to the kitchen. I feel my cheeks redden, and I rub my right eye, which after a few days' respite, is irritated once again.

CHAPTER 10

We climbed into the car with two small bags and no idea where we were going. We ate fish in the only open restaurant of Porto Garibaldi, looking through the glass door at boats with female names cocooned in fog. In the middle of the night, we lay on the soft mattress of a huge bed in a hotel on the Lido delle Nazioni. Our window opened onto a swimming pool full of slides and trampolines, and heaps of leaves at the bottom.

"You've been here before?"

"Yes, as a little girl, one summer."

Memories of wave wars on the lake, my mother, exhausted and smiling, on a wooden bench. Ada and I ate ice cream and threw coins in the juke-box of the little bar that faced the waterfront. Melancholy did not yet exist for us, not even to see our mother leave the bench and shut herself inside a phone booth to call someone.

We made love in room 28, stopping and starting, and all the words we spoke were rough and drowsy.

The next day, we woke up late and paid for the room.

A stay on the beach on a gray and windy Sunday, where I thought again of the motorboat Delphinus, which used to pick up people for a trip to the mouth of the Po, scattering threads of music from a megaphone and offering wine and bluefish for twenty-thousand lire. Ada and I would love to have gone on that trip, but our mother wouldn't let us.

The fear has suddenly returned — that thing I have to reckon with as soon as I feel a little attached or in tune with someone.

"People get hurt doing things like this," I said to him.

He tightened the red scarf around his neck, and he looked at the sea without saying anything. I pulled him by the sleeve of his tweed jacket.

"What's the matter?" he asked me.

"Nothing."

Andrea Berti placed two cold fingers on top of mine, and I scooted away. "Shall we go?"

The weekend is over. "See you tomorrow," Andrea tells me in the doorway. I hesitate as he extends his mouth for a kiss. Then I go down two flights of stairs without thinking of anything. In the street, blasts of rain make me gasp all the way to my car. I climb in and turn on the wipers. Rain drums on the roof of the Citroën.

I pass by a row of night clubs, and at the corner of Via Saffi I see a knot of people: three men are holding back a man who's brandishing a bottle at a fat, balding guy. I slow down, I lean out the car window, and I can't believe my eyes: the elegant Alessandro Dazi sits beaten and bloody on the curb side.

I leave the car and push through the crowd. Dazi grabs my hand and gets up off the ground. He has a busted jaw, black eyes, and can barely stand on his feet.

"What the hell were you thinking?" I shout as soon as we get in the car.

He's completely smashed and mumbles incomprehensible sentences. I hand him a tissue, glancing at the progress of the quarrel through my rear-view mirror, then I start the engine.

As I drive him back to his house, he talks to me in a drunken delirium about his second divorce and the chain of pizzerias that he's ruined. The air inside reeks from his breath. He opens the car door in front of 12 Via Guerrazzi and says: "Doctor, I've been meaning to say this to you for a while… You remind me of a girl, a friend of Angela."

He's about to leave, but I hold him back. "What was her name?"

He fumbles with the rain-soaked belt of his overcoat and doesn't answer.

I raise my voice and repeat: "What was her name?"

He looks at himself in the little mirror and starts to act coy. "I'm really in bad shape," he rasps as he touches his jaw.

I shake him hard. "Ada? Did she call herself Ada?"

"Ada? It's a nice name…"

I shove him out of the Citroën, and he falls on the wet asphalt.

I get out of the car. "Dazi, listen to me closely," I say menacingly. "When you lived in Rome, did you ever meet a certain Ada Cantini?"

He sneezes and repeats my sister's name like a nursery rhyme. "Ada…Ada… Ada…"

I wipe my face with the sleeve of my jacket. "You'll catch pneumonia."

He opens his eyes and stares at me. "You too."

I leave him there and climb back into the car.

I wake up late — past eleven — feeling as though I never fell into a deep sleep. I don't know if the rain from last night or something else makes me feel so rotten with my throat on fire and my bones like icicles.

I get up, put on some clothes, and realize it's too late for breakfast: I only want a drink. I climb into the car, and after a few yards I stop in front of the church of San Giuseppe Lavoratore.

I go inside. I start to smile because it sounds a bit like an atheist's prayer, someone who can't get rid of her skepticism but can't survive without lying to herself now and then. I use up my limited fund of illusions as I light two candles for a euro a piece.

I think back to how furious I was to see Ada in the mortuary room, her arms crossed like a good little girl. The only thing I wanted to say to her was: "I hope you didn't kill yourself because of some rejection…"

(But what do I know? I haven't read enough Dostoyevski to be able to understand suicide. The only thing I know is that death makes people smaller. In the coffin, my sister seems to have lost a good six inches.)

It's noon when I step inside a bar on Via Rizzoli that has a wooden counter top lined with bowls of cold pasta and appetizers. Young people and not-so-young people, perched on stools, drink their aperitifs and reach for little squares of pizza and triangles of bread garnished with sauces. I sit down with my gin bitter and feel chills throughout my entire body.

If love has arrived…fine, I have all the symptoms. Love. A need I've always set aside. Something I've always considered incompatible with me like an extreme sport — from too much ego, from fear of emptiness, from not wanting to hear anyone ever say: "She is, was, or will be mine." No, it's not true. I'm having an affair with Tim's professor. "An amorous friendship," as the French would say. Yes, it sounds less sentimental that way.

I'm not in the mood to do anything at the office today, so I decide to look up an old case in order to distract myself and pass the time. Among so many files, one in particular sticks out; it belongs to Giulia Manzoni, a woman from Pesaro who knocked on my door some years ago. She was married to a high-school gym teacher and had a six-year-old son. I recall her sitting in the arm chair, faded and small, with straw blond hair and large sunglasses that covered part of her face. She expressed herself succinctly in a few dry sentences: her husband beat her, and she was afraid that, sooner or later, he would start in on the boy.

She didn't want my pity, and she hadn't gone to the police because she didn't care to end up in a room with someone photographing the bruises on her breasts and the knife marks left by her husband during their bouts of sex.

Giulia Manzoni had to overcome her sense of shame and realize that the police should handle her problem. She won her battle: the unsuspecting husband was arrested, and the wife moved with her son to her sister's house in Trebbo di Reno. I had Luca Bruni and his officers to thank for this.

The last time I saw her, she seemed to have lost her anxiety — an anxiety she had defined as "constitutional." Instead, she stood there rigid and lifeless, with a fixed look on her face, like someone who had no reason to live. A month later, a newspaper article mentioned her plunge into the Reno River and the recovery of her body.

I put the photo of Giulia Manzoni back in the folder with the other documents, and I ask myself why I keep it. I'd like to call Andrea, but he's probably teaching right now and won't return home for an hour or so. I think about it. It's much stronger than I am: the fear that he'll exit from my life as suddenly as he entered it.

The day comes to mind when our house was full of relatives and carabinieri, eating and drinking. Ada was playing Gounod's "Ave Maria" on the piano, while my father, in a dark suit, was talking to a retired colleague. I drew near to hear what they were saying. "She left us," my father kept repeating and nodding, and there was nothing else to say, except to confirm: she, my mother, had left us. It seemed to me a strange, curious word, considering that it also had another meaning. It made me think of my mother as a woman floating away who has cut the cord. I hoped then, with all my might, that dying and leaving were different things and that she was somewhere else at that moment, in a safe refuge, on a whim or a calculated plan, and that one day or another a post card would arrive, sending us her greetings.

The phone rings.

"Did you know, they've shoved her pictures right in my face," Lattice shouts at the other end of the line. And they asked me if I knew my wife's lovers. The plan was..."

"What plan?"

"My plan, Mrs. Cantini. To strangle one of those bastards!"

"Does Bruni know this?"

"I'm talking about impulses, you understand?"

I'm confused, as if an important detail was escaping me. "Was it you, Lattice? Did you kill Donatella?"

"You call her by her first name, and yet you never knew her. What gives you the right?"

My tone hardens. "I'll never know her now — that's for sure."

I hear him panting, and I imagine him on the bed of his squalid apartment, sweaty hand on the receiver, a raw bundle of nerves and impaired mental faculties.

"I find them everywhere, they check on me, in front of the house, at the club, even at the funeral they didn't let me cry in peace…"

"They're doing their job."

"But do they know anything about how much I loved my wife? How sweet she was when I first met her? I never made her work, you know. I treated her like a lady. I wanted children and she didn't. She said that they'd grow up in an ugly environment, that I'd come home at five in the morning, that sooner or later they'd shut down the Cocorito and we'd end up on our butts, not a dime to our name. Utter crap. There was plenty of money. She never lacked for anything. You saw her, right? Always beautiful and well-groomed. Yes, beautiful for someone else because — chump that I am — there were months I didn't touch her, that I accepted her endless periods, her head aches…"

I'm at my limit. "Yes, I understand."

"What do you mean, understand?"

"Did you never cheat on her?"

"No. Yes… For a man, it's different."

"Explain that to me."

He loses it. "Why don't you explain something to me? Why do people change? Why did my wife become a stranger from one day to the next?"

With that, Lattice bangs down the receiver and cuts off communication. I'm not offended, but I ask myself if it's time to talk to Bruni. I haven't heard from him in a few days. Maybe he doesn't have news for me, but then again, he got what he wanted: the photos.

The photos Lattice obsesses over.

The photos in my computer.

Curiosity drives me to open the files of pictures I took when Mrs. Verze was still alive. The moments in the life of a woman without any more guard dogs, finally free to enjoy the second half of her life just as she likes. I click and look at her. There's a man with a beard at her side. They're leaving a leather goods shop. I click on another picture. She's with a boy about Tim's age; he whispers something in her ear with an air of complicity. In another picture, instead, the man is somewhat older than her. I click on the last picture and sit stone still.

The man next to Donatella, with a strong profile and dark hair, whom I see from behind, slightly out of focus... it's Alessandro Dazi. I enlarge the image to make sure, then I pick up the phone.

"We've questioned him," Bruni tells me a few minutes later.

"Strange coincidence, don't you think?"

"That he's also come onto you?"

"Yes."

"He says he slept with Mrs. Verze only a few times. They went to the same gym."

Two hours later.

"I'm not used to it," I tell him softly, naked under the gray sheets of his bed.

"Is that a compliment?" he says after a while.

(I like these silences between one sentence and another.)

I plump up the pillow and lean it against the headboard. "Perhaps I'm suggesting something."

"We're here, and we know each other."

I look at him. "It looks like a normal thing."

"And that's good, don't you think?"

I nod with an indecisive smile, and not because being here isn't great, but because there's something urging me to rise up, get dressed, and go back to my old ways.

"Let's give up our doubts and fears," Andrea says as he hands me my tights.

He moves through the room, naked and pale, with the relaxed posture of someone who doesn't care if he looks scrawny even with his clothes on. I believe he's right: that we can offer each other something more than our heavy hearts and bad ironies. I get up and hug him from behind with my arms around his sweaty stomach. He opens his mouth as if he's about to say something, but then turns around and silently kisses my shoulder.

Aunt Lidia lives in an apartment in the neighborhood of Cirenaica, not far from where my father now lives. She does his housekeeping, and every other day brings him pans of meatballs and baked pasta, which he puts in the fridge and eats by himself when he remembers.

She lives with three big lazy cats. She has never married, and my sister and I have never liked her very much. Mama considered her a cold woman, practical and authoritarian. Whenever Mama met her at the front door, she would hide her hands behind her back and crack her fingers nervously.

Lidia Cantini used to laugh about the permissive upbringing that my mother gave my sister. "You need a backbone to deal with that girl," she said and proposed a convent school run by nuns to straighten out the little rebel of the house. When my aunt peppered her words with dialect, Mama would retaliate with expressions like "Mais c'est une folie!" to emphasize the difference between her (a cultivated woman who read the novels of Françoise Sagan in French) and my aunt, who responded to these outbursts in a foreign language with an acid smile and a sigh of reproof.

As I knock at the door — I called yesterday to let her know about my visit — I picture the guarded expression with which my mother looked at her and the soft, elegant gestures of her hand when she reassured Ada that the story of the convent was just the harmless jest or "boutade" of an old maid.

Aunt Lidia is seventy, with short white hair, a long pointed nose, and a small mouth. A pair of black piercing eyes, undimmed by old age, sparkle in her wrinkled face.

The tiny living room is orderly and clean. Two cats lie asleep on a leather arm chair, a third one, black, follows my aunt into the kitchen with a hungry whine. "I've made tea," I hear her say in her contralto voice. I sit on a stiff-back sofa with cat hairs all over the flower print upholstery. Wind from a half-open window stirs the curtains. I decide not to take off my jacket so I won't freeze to death.

My aunt places a tray on the table arranged with two cups full of yellow liquid, a sugar bowl, and a plate of hard dry cookies. On a walnut side table, next to a photo of my father in uniform, is another photo of my sister astride her beloved white Piaggio. "She loved that scooter like a dog. Remember how much she cried when they stole it," my aunt adds as she follows my look.

"Aunt, by any chance have you saved some of Ada's things?"

She raises her thin eyebrows and, despite her age, maintains a straight posture. "There could be something in the basement, if you're not afraid of mice. But first drink your tea."

I sip the tasteless beverage in silence.

"What's the matter? Are you discouraged?" she asks while studying me closely. "What a foolish venture to open up that shabby agency..."

"I'm going down to the basement," I tell her.

She mutters something as she hands me the keys.

The stink of rat poison hits me right away, and when I turn on the basement light, I'm more afraid of roaches than of mice. My aunt told me that under the canary cage, next to a rusty Graziella bicycle, there are boxes full of clothes and other junk. I move aside some bottles, a water mattress, old-fashioned hats, and I find a metal trunk, long and rectangular, that somehow looks familiar. I open it.

Objects are concrete reminders, and the memory that you've lost — or think you've lost — knocks you off balance. It just takes a little Ken Scott purse for you to see Ada at the Mercato Piazzola. The night before, you went to a debate on Vietnam with your pals from the soccer federation, while she was watching *The Chairs* by Ionesco at the conference center, where she met a girl who was taking a course in acting, diction, and stage production. As she rummaged through the stalls of silk blouses, necklaces, and vests, she said to you, "Giorgia, I'd really like to act in a theatre company."

I take her school photo from the trunk: Ada laughing in the arms of a scrawny, bespectacled classmate. Then the postcard of Monterosso. She went there on a school trip where a girlfriend saw her making out with Masi, her science teacher, during the twelve-mile route of the Via dell' Amore. Fortunately, my father knew nothing about it.

There it is: *EroZero* by Renato Zero. She was crazy about that record. I'd put on an album by Genesis, and she would take it off. I'd tease her by calling her "groupy!"

The photos of her trip to Malta. Summer 1980. Ada stretched out on the pink beach on the island of Gozo.

A Roberta di Camerino black-and-yellow checkered scarf.

The lyrics of a popular song by Vendetti, "Roma Capoccia."

The first three pages of a novel she had started to write, with the title *My Lair*.

The score of Rachmaninov's *Prelude*.

The photo of a three-year-old boy whom she babysat for a while.

The movie poster of *Suspiria* by Dario Argento. We saw it together, and Ada swooned, or pretended to, when she recalled how much attention they paid to costuming and direction.

She liked horror movies. I recall how she'd squirm with excitement as she helped out in the projection room for *Watch Me When I Kill* or *Carrie, The Look of Satan*. She liked guys who rode blue Vespas. She liked Altero's pizzas and Pino's ice cream. She never gained weight.

A Latin book covered in dust. One year she had to repeat a grade…

I replace everything in the trunk.

"Find anything?"

Aunt Lidia is sitting in an armchair with a plaid blanket on her knees. She passes a hand over her leg complaining about arthritis. "What agony…"

I take a seat on the sofa, between a cushion and a gray-and-white cat. I sneeze and think about my allergy.

"Your sister always used to say that nobody loved her. My god, how she liked to play the victim..."

I lean my head to the side, start to sulk, and grip my knees, waiting to dart up and get away from here.

"'Think,' your father would say to her. 'Think!' It didn't matter. She was pure instinct like an animal." She hugs one of her cats. "You were different."

I sink my head between my shoulders. "What was I like, Aunt?"

She smiles as she scratches her jutting chin. "You didn't dance around the maypole."

"Come again?"

She stops smiling. "You knew how to control your emotions."

(Aunt Lidia: a woman whom no one has ever dared to contradict.)

Afraid the conversation will turn from Ada to my mother, I thank her for the tea and tell her I've got work to do in the office.

"I apologize for not walking you to the door, but the humidity..."

"It's not good for you to have the heat turned off and the window open."

"The cold is bracing."

I go up to her and bend down. She plants a wet kiss on my brow. "Come back, won't you...maybe with your dad..."

I shut the door softly behind me.

In front of Marconi Elementary School, there's a small tree-lined piazza with a closed up ice-cream stand and a little fountain.

I'm so tired I end up stretched out on a park bench like a bum with my red eye turned up to the sky, dense and colorless like a milk carton.

The voice of Alessandro Dazi brings me back to earth, so I get up and make room for him on the bench. He stands there fixed, not knowing what to say, but at last he sits down.

"I'm a spendthrift, do you know that? I've just paid an astronomical amount for this pair of shoes."

For a few moments we both look at the shoes he's wearing.

"I must apologize to you...for that stupid quarrel. I was drunk."

"You had a good reason to drink."

"Oh yes," he sighs theatrically. "Angela. Look over there," he adds pointing to a maple tree. "Trees strip in the winter and put on clothes again in the summer. We do the exact opposite. Have you ever thought about it?"

I light up a Camel. "I'm not here to talk about nature, Dazi, but about Donatella Verze or Lattice, if you prefer. What name did you know her by?"

He takes off his leather gloves. "What do you want to know?"

"Everything."

"It's so banal."

"I adore banality."

"Fine," he sighs again. "I noticed her at the gym. She sweated when she worked out. Perfect physique. We chatted in front of the drink machine, and half an hour later we were performing a different kind of gymnastic routine in my bedroom. A great fuck. That's it."

"Yes, that's it. And now she's dead."

"I've already told the officer who questioned me what I know. Are you interested in the case?"

Hordes of children file out of the school gate. Fathers and mothers wait for them with weary faces in double-parked cars.

"Don't ask me if I know that woman. I like to have affairs, Doctor, I'm vain, I hate an empty bed, and I have no imagination."

I stare at the half-lit cigarette butt at my feet, unsure whether to give it a final crush with my heel. I get up from the bench, and as I walk away I hear Dazi's voice: "Where are you going? Wait up. I still have to pay you for..."

The decision to have a massage was lightning fast. There's an aesthetician center near the office. I often pass by it with an air of superiority, but as I step inside, I realize now's the time for a recuperation plan.

The girl assigned to me comes up and asks me to get undressed and stretch out on the table. Her name is Roberta. She has black hair tied back in a ponytail, a sweet manner, and a strong Sicilian accent.

I close my eyes and feel her oily hands attack my taut body. She stops torturing me now and then to wipe the sweat from her brow with the inside of her elbow. At a certain point, she breaks the silence and tells me that she's been married for three months and that her husband, a mason, is from Palermo just like her. Then comes the question I was dreading: "Are you married?"

"No. I've been living for several years with…"

It's a lie that evidently reassures her, since she gives me a satisfied smile without interrupting my massage.

"So many women come here," she tells me in a confidential tone, "over forty, single, and childless. They don't know how to spend their time and who to talk with…I think they're unhappy women."

I close my eyes and the conversation, glad to have invented another life so as not to disillusion Roberta, and I lose myself thinking about Donatella Verze and her joyous forty years, leaving the fashion boutiques with bags full of clothes, euphoric over her new status as an independent woman who hasn't yielded to depression and regret. But I don't bring up Donatella because I don't want to risk hearing that she deserved an end like that.

I climb off the table and get dressed. Roberta explains to me that I should take at least twenty more sessions if I want to achieve visible results. I thank her for the advice and promise to think about it.

CHAPTER 12

"You have to find him, understand? You have to find him! You have to go there, to Bolzano, and bring him back here, to my house, dead or alive!"

The crazy woman in front of me is Germana Bonini. She's fifty-five and sounds like a strident vendor at the market.

I'm baffled. This woman's face changes expression constantly. She sits on the edge of the arm chair, crossing and uncrossing her short, stubby legs — her cheeks drawn up into a diabolical smile. Same old story. The husband has run away with a woman twenty years younger, leaving the wife to deal with the bar, the bills, and the kids, all alone.

She has big bones and heavy jowls, with a smear of lipstick across her heart-shaped mouth. She's domineering and knows exactly why she's here and what she expects from me.

I must say I feel some sympathy for these women warriors armed with willpower and bad taste, indifferent to what other people think — hysterical revolutionaries who bray their rights of ownership and who defend themselves, if necessary, in a theatrical and surgical manner.

"I'd go to Bolzano myself if I didn't have the bar and three useless kids to look after. Me, the Nazi! That's what my husband calls me. Oh, it made life easy for him to marry someone like me, someone who takes care of everything, who fixes problems, who raises children to the sound of slaps, good old-fashioned slaps! Meanwhile, he runs around or plays cards with customers or goes after some neighborhood tramp, maybe even pays for her groceries!"

"I can try," I bleat softly, "but I don't guarantee…"

"If you bring him back to me," she says grinding her teeth and talking about her husband as she would about a dog that got lost, "I promise you'll be richly rewarded!" She tosses her head and sighs. "I was a cabaret singer when I met him. You know how nice it is to marry someone your own age? You've grown up listening to the same songs, and these are things that never let you down, things that a younger woman just can't give you. Roots, values, whatever you want to call them."

I have no intention of contradicting her. "Why did you stop singing?"

"My dear, you can do some things when you're young, like touring with an orchestra from one Unity Festival to another, sea-side resorts, dance halls, but when the kids come..."

"I understand."

"I was Germana, the lead singer of the Manni di Budrio Band, and all the band leaders pursued me. As a young man, Walter was strong as a bull and kind of roguishly charming. So I married him and made him manager of the band. When the children were born, we got the bar and gave up the polkas and mazurkas. What else could we do? It all went fine for fifteen years, then rumor spread that he had a girlfriend. I couldn't see straight. In front of everybody, I spat right in his face — a masterpiece. And I took him back. But this time he went away at night, and I take a sleeping pill, so I didn't hear him..." She removes a piece of paper from her purse and waves it under my nose. "It's the first draft of a letter..." She starts to read: "Dearest Lilli, you are the strong sun that scorches the old grass, the champagne bottle in the silver bucket, the golden candle that sets fire to my volcano..." She crumples up the paper. "Hear what a poet he is? At sixty, he wants to spend the rest of his life with her! What should we call it, senile dementia?"

Two hours on the road, a stop at the autogrill for a dish of gnocchi alla Tirolese and piece of strudel, and I go to sleep in a room of the Albergo Regina. All this after passing Verona, then Trento, glancing at the River Adige and realizing that the mountains still give me a sense of claustrophobia, which I've had since I was a child.

I wake up early, ready to hunt down the deserter. In Via Goethe, at eight in the morning, the pubs are full of beer drinkers. I go into a tobacco shop that has a souvenir display case, the kind with glass boots, laughing cable cars, cuckoo clocks, and little alpine feather-cap key chains. Exactly at nine, I'm outside Walter Bonini's house, holding a photo of Germana and him on their wedding day.

Twenty minutes and six Camels later, a large fat man opens wide the wooden door to the small building. He's seen me from the window walking back and forth, smoking one cigarette after another, and has obviously wondered who I am. I briefly give him the gist of things, and he, in a good-natured, almost timid way, smoothing his gleaming black mustache, asks me if I'd like to take a little stroll.

As I foresaw, Walter Bonini isn't interested in hearing about returning home. He says he's happy here, and his wife can do what she wants, send the cops after him, the father- and mother-in-law, the brothers-in-law, but he will never move from Bolzano. He can breathe here. He's joined the German party, takes part in politics, and has even become bilingual. And then there's Liliana, or Lilli, who has made him feel alive again.

"It's not that I don't love my wife anymore. But since I've been here, I see things in a more objective light. It may be the air or the mountains, I don't know. I wouldn't have any purpose in life without Germana, and she's so great with the kids, but those women who don't give you enough space…"

(I guessed as much.)

"I needed to feel like a man again. I'm not sure if you know what I mean. But that's not the only thing. Lilli listens to me, she's full of enthusiasm, and she's a dancer…"

I almost ask him if she does lap dances. But he clarifies: "Classical," cutting short the idea I had formed. "Tonight she's performing the *The Dying Swan*. Do you want to see her?"

"No thanks," I answer. "I can't stand people who are always on their toes."

He laughs heartily and slaps me on the shoulder.

"A young woman is a miracle cure for a man with a past, and I," he adds, "believe me — call me an egoist — but I've jumped on this train with all the euphoria of a young boy. Mainly because I was sick to death of staying on the margins of everything, of being ordered around by my wife, by my children, even by my customers. But above all, dear Mrs. Cantini…"

"Giorgia. Call me Giorgia."

"Giorgia…I was tired of having memories."

He turns around, and we head back toward his house.

"I realize it was a crazy thing to do."

"Do you have a strong heart, Bonini?"

He thumps his chest and laughs. "And if not?"

I pay for the hotel room and get on the road right away. In two hours I'll be back home. I hope Germana Bonini at least pays for the gas.

As soon as I reach Bologna, I leave a phone message for Andrea. Even if I'm tired and sleep-deprived, I have no desire to stay at home, so I park the Citroën in Via San Vitale and walk to Piazza Maggiore, devouring a slice of pizza.

As I sit on the stairs of the Chiesa di San Petronio, I light a Camel and look at the piazza. Soon a rust-colored dog comes up and nuzzles me. He's nature's practical joke — a kind of multi-ethnic mutt.

"Hi there, handsome," I say to him. "Oh, you're not really handsome. Sorry, no offense, but you're a nice guy."

He stares at me with commanding eyes. He has canine pride, not the docile and submissive eyes you often associate with un-pedigreed dogs. His owner calls him back with a whistle, and the dog dashes to the center of the piazza, winding between the skinny legs of a young punker.

I light another Camel and fade out. Weariness.

Dementia, they call it. I read about this word in the dictionary one day. I like the sound it makes when you say it out loud. Dementia: mental confusion, disorientation. It's a great name for a disease.

I wonder if the solitude of Andrea Berti is solid and compact like mine. I wonder if he really wants to give up some of it to make room for me. I wonder if I should ask him something about the women he's been with. Things never change, Giorgia.

I'm twenty-four, sitting at a little table in a tavern on Via dei Poeti, drinking a beer with Gianluca, a former college buddy of mine, and listening to him talk about a woman who wasn't me.

Gianluca was nothing special. He had an enormous nose, dissonant like a wrong chord. The rest of his face was perfectly regular, but that nose of his spoiled the harmony. I liked his brains, how he thought, and above all, the way he talked about Sara, the fact that he loved her and felt that loving someone is better and more important than being lovers.

As he looks at me and thinks of her, I ask myself: "How long will this night of ours in the tavern last? How will I feel when we leave here, and he climbs on his Due Cavalli scooter and rides off to Sara's place?"

After Gianluca, I always wondered if getting involved with men who were already taken wasn't just a way of continuing to be alone with my ghosts.

A few drops begin to fall. I get up. Hurrying towards my car, I ask myself why Andrea Berti hasn't called me back.

In the car, I call the Kiki Bar and ask for Germana. I have no desire to let her know how things went in Bolzano, but I have to do it. It's my job. She pays me for this. Soon one of her kids comes back to the phone and says their mother isn't there. I leave my name and say I'll call again.

CHAPTER 13

This is how you dance the Tango, dance the Tango, dance the Tango…

I'm on the sofa, and this line of Ada's keeps buzzing in my head. Surely, she was referring to *Last Tango in Paris*. I've seen that movie, too, ages ago. *We saw it for the third time. Now I know all the lines by heart…*

I can't remember if I liked it or not when I saw it. Let's say it wasn't one of my favorite films.

Anyway, I'm not sleepy.

I go to the closet, take out the shoe box, and scatter Ada's letters on the parquet floor. Then I look at them for the umpteenth time the way you'd look at a riddle with no solution.

I should get a good night's sleep, gather my strength, and call Andrea again to find out whether he's still alive. Instead, I grab my windbreaker from the coat hook behind the door and go out again. There's one last thing for me to do.

When I arrive at the video rental store a few steps from my house, I take the card from my wallet and insert it in the slot, then push the RENT VHS button and choose among various genres they offer me: romance, action, drama… This kind of film can't be fashionable nowadays, and most likely the store doesn't carry it. But no, there it is: an old cult film that caused a scandal back in its time. I make my selection and wait for the videocassette to slide directly into my hands.

Before I start the video player, I go into the kitchen, grab another can of beer, and open a new pack of Camels. Sitting on the sofa, with my legs crossed, I press PLAY on the remote and begin watching.

On the screen is Marlon Brando with that seen-it-all, done-it-all look of the forty-something man who has a thousand identities. In front of the bed where his wife lies dead from suicide, he says: "I don't understand why you did it. I'd have done it, too, if I'd known you were going to." She, the wife, had another man, Massimo Girotti, who gave them both the same bathrobe as a present.

I fast forward the tape. Marlon is leaning against the wall. Maria Schneider, skinny and curly-haired, sits on a mattress and takes off her shoes. After a while, Marlon says to her: "You're all alone, and you can't free yourself from this feeling of complete solitude, not until you look death in the face."

My eyes are closing from sleep. She's walking, while he follows at a distance. "Quo vadis, baby?" he says as he draws near.

I fast forward the tape. He: "The best fucks are the ones you can do only here, in this apartment." I finish the beer, put it on the table, and stop then and there, frozen for a few moments.

I rewind the tape.

Maria is walking. Marlon is behind her.

"Quo vadis, baby?"

I turn and see Andrea Berti smiling outside the Trattoria Trebbi. "Quo vadis, baby?"

It's four in the morning when I get in the car like an automaton and drive quickly through the half-deserted streets, whitened by snowflakes soft as flour. It's 4:12 when he opens the door, sleepy in his pajamas and says: "Hi, come on in," smiling like an old friend who's ready to take out the pieces for a game of chess.

I hesitate on the door mat and move backwards, then watch my hand as it rises and strikes: the mark of my five fingers is printed on his incredulous face.

We've seen each other naked to the bone, but now he pulls a sweater over his pajama top. A. sits on the bed. I smoke at the window while the sky is clear outside and the falling snow seems like Christmas.

I listen to his story as if it came from another room or as if my hearing were suddenly impaired. I hear him talk in a passionless, neutral tone that consumes me with rage, and I realize I've always known it.

Andrea Berti was young back then. He wanted to be an actor, but then he graduated from the university with a thesis on the cinema of Bernardo Bertolucci. He had met Ada at an audition, and she was just one of many actresses he fucked during this stage in his life. Yes, he saw that movie with Ada a few times. For him, *Last Tango in Paris* was only a chapter in his thesis. Yes, Giulio wasn't there that night, and they had two bottles of whiskey and a few grams of coke. After they had sex, Ada started to laugh and said: "I'm going to kill myself. Do you think I can't do it?" "No, you won't do it," he answered her.

She wobbled as she climbed onto a chair, still laughing, and wrapped the leather strap of her purse around her neck and tied it tightly to a rafter in the ceiling. He couldn't keep his eyes open, his vision was cloudy, and he was about to vomit. His head fell to the table with a heavy thud, and in a few minutes he was fast asleep.

Then he woke up startled: the phone was ringing, and Giulio's voice was on the message machine: "Ada…you're probably sleeping…I wanted to tell you that I'll be there around noon." Sunlight was entering through cracks in the shutters. He got up, approached Ada's body, and touched her leg. He was twenty-three and had never seen a corpse in his life, but he knew that my sister was dead, indisputably dead. So he closed his eyes and opened them again. He opened and closed them many times because he didn't believe what he was seeing. The French call it a "cauchemar," he tells me. It seemed like a nightmare. Instead it was reality.

That corpse was too far gone, too hideous, for him to take down from the rafter, to feel for a pulse, to try and revive it. (He doesn't say it, but that's what he did, or rather what he didn't do.)

Seized by panic, he washed out the glass he'd been drinking from and put six Marlboro butts in the pocket of his leather jacket (Ada smoked Muratti), then he left. As he descended the staircase, he met an old man leading a large dog (a griffon) on a leash.

How long did it take her to die? What did she feel? How much did she suffer, and what kind of pain? Was the pain only physical at that point? Did she wonder for a fraction of a second: "What the fuck am I doing?" Did she search for a handhold? And for how long did she try? Life and death. At first, you're there, and then you're not. All it takes is one action.

I feel the cat rub up against my pants leg, a hungry cat complaining about its empty bowl. A. talks about the vanity of actors like my sister, who prepare for auditions by listening to the opera *Falstaff* because, according to her, the music of Verdi could touch all the strings of her soul. He isn't able to look me in the face, but he needs to make it clear that he didn't know who I was when he saw me at Tim's party. I think he realized it later, however. He says he didn't say anything then because it wasn't easy to admit. I hurl myself at him, and he doesn't react, but the pain I'm feeling slows down my movements, strips away their flesh and bone, and I know I won't leave a bruise on him.

"She wanted success," he spits out in a low voice.

"She also wanted you," I say coldly. "I've read her letters."

He shakes his head, staring at the wall poster of an Edward Hopper painting, and sighs deeply. "She slept with directors, producers, with whoever promised her a part…"

I head toward the door.

"I didn't tell her to do it," he says to justify himself.

"But you were there when she hanged herself."

I go into the kitchen to drink a glass of water, and A. follows me. For him, Ada was just a crazy girl who flashed across his life, leaving an ugly memory behind, until the day when chance or destiny made him rediscover her at a party by the way I moved, by some physical detail, by some inflection of my voice, and after sixteen years he saw her flickering again in the void. I can't believe that I've made love with this man. I feel like throwing myself on the floor and dying. (Are only my mother and sister allowed to die? Why not me? Why not my father?)

I still taste the flavor of his tongue on my palate. I'd like to demolish all the furniture in his apartment, break everything to bits and pieces, and instead I'm rigid, immobile, and feel like a dirty rag.

"What fucking movie is this?" I say to him.

He blinks and takes a breath. "If it were possible to go back…"

"What would you do, tell me?"

He takes a cigarette from my pack and lights it. (Good, you've started smoking again.) "Giorgia, we were young…"

"Did you ever beat her?"

"I gave her a slap, just once, at a party."

"Why?"

"She was drunk and acting like an idiot with a director she was negotiating with for a part. Ada used to drink a lot."

I smirk. "But not you."

"Yes, me too," he admits. Now his tone of voice is hard.

"You really should have become an actor."

He smiles bitterly. "I'm sorry."

"Why didn't you help her?"

"Giulio was her man."

(Ah, Giulio. Another guy who didn't understand anything.)

"Who was Anna?"

"Anna Parisi? A friend of hers."

"Did they borrow each other's clothes? Did they go to the movies together?"

He rubs his forehead. "No, I think they did other things."

The cat comes to the door with me. I shut it behind me sharply. When I walk down to the street, the sun is shining and people are shoveling piles of snow. I hear someone say, "Luckily, not much has fallen." Except for the children, everyone hopes it will start to rain so the snow won't freeze and they can begin driving again without trouble.

Chapter 14

At home I set the alarm with the idea of sleeping a few hours. Impossible.

I huddle, still dressed, in a corner of my bed in the dark. I turn to one side. My right arm, which has gone to sleep under my head, starts to tingle annoyingly. A cold shower won't be enough to remove the smell of this man who used to fuck my sister sixteen years ago. There's something about his story that isn't right, and I don't know what it is. I studied Marcus Aurelius in high school. "A person who does wrong to someone else also wrongs himself." Is that good enough for me?

At nine-thirty I go into the office with tangled hair and a top that reeks of sweat. Lucio looks at me and realizes immediately that I've had a night without sleep. My expression is not inviting, and he avoids asking me questions.

I go into the office, leave the door open, and begin to pace up and down the room. "Tim?"

Spasimo answers from his bunker. "He hasn't shown up."

"I'm tired. I'm going home."

"What did you say?"

I raise my voice. "I said I'm leaving."

"But you just...all right. If Tim comes by, what should I tell him?"

"Nothing."

"What?"

"Nothing. Don't say anything to him."

"I get it!"

I pass in front of his half-open door. "Bye."

He keeps staring at the computer. "Bye."

I lower my head and scrape my shoe against the door frame, unsure whether to go in or not.

I hear him say: "Did you notice it snowed last night?"

"There's snow everywhere. I'm not blind, you know."

"I was just making a remark."

I open the door all the way. "Lucio…"

"Yes," he says without turning around.

"Would you care to have dinner at my place tonight?"

"What are you cooking?"

"I was thinking…filet of sole and mashed potatoes. What do you say?"

"And dessert?" He underlines this.

"Dessert too. Chocolate mousse."

Finally, he looks at me. "Eight o'clock?"

"Yes. Just bring some wine."

Next to my car, sitting on the seat of his scooter, is Tim. Standing close to him is Gaia. I stop a safe distance away and watch them exchange a kiss straight out of the romantic film *The Party*. My stomach burns, and my throat stings; I wonder if I have sodium bicarbonate at home.

As I approach, Tim turns the key. "Your eye is really red, boss." I see him leave, balanced on one wheel, addressing a "later, baby" to his new girlfriend. The euphoria on Gaia's face is more contained, but she smiles, too, and asks me if I'd like to go to a bar on Via Zamboni where they make fabulous appetizers.

"I'm not very hungry," I confess.

"But I am," she replies.

"Get in," I tell her, opening the car door.

As I drive there, I try to keep my eyes open, while Gaia tells me about the Irish Pub that she and Tim went to last night. After a few red beers, he put his arm around her shoulders and gave her a kiss. Afterwards, they ended up at his place and made love.

"We're happy now," she says, "but it won't last."

"Why?"

"Because love affairs come to an end."

I jam the gear shift. "Not all of them."

"They end because we die," she explains.

"You're only eighteen, Gaia. Isn't it a bit soon…"

"Better to think about these things while there's time."

"My god, what traffic," I sigh.

She looks out the window. "One day all these people will die. Even the Towers of Bologna will collapse."

The Towers appear before me as I search for a parking spot. "Let's hope not now… It's a good thing you're in love."

After we each have an appetizer, Gaia and I say good bye in front of the Feltrinelli bookstore. She wants to buy the plays of Sarah Kane. I have to return home to make dinner for Spasimo.

I get back in the car.

I don't know if it's a coincidence or a sign of destiny, but what I see, stopped at a traffic light on Via Oriani, staggers my imagination. My father is standing next to a lamp post. Behind him: a bar, a tobacco shop, and a flower store. He's talking to a man.

That man is Andrea Berti.

The light turns green, I wait to change gears, but I'm immediately blasted by a horn from a mini-car. I move forward slowly as I glance in the rear-view mirror. They're still talking.

They know each other.

Andrea Berti and my father know each other.

I go into Enzo's bar and order a gin bitter. Enzo asks me if I've run into a gust of wind, and I know he's referring to my red eye. "It's just stress," I answer.

"The living dead," he says.

I could introduce him to Gaia, if she didn't already have a boyfriend.

I let some time pass, about an hour, then I decide to phone Andrea Berti. He doesn't have a cell, so I call him at home.

I get the answering machine, and I'd rather not leave a message.

I call the office to vent with Lucio, but my father answers. "What are you doing there?"

He's stunned by the question. This, he reminds me, is his agency.

I assume a casual tone. "Do you happen to know a certain Andrea Berti?"

Silence.

Then: "Yes."

"How is that?"

"I saw him one time at Rome; he was a friend of your sister."

"And so?"

"And so nothing, Giorgia. He's a pleasant person. Ever since he moved here to live in Bologna, he calls me now and then to ask how I'm doing."

"And you see each other?"

"On occasion, yes, for coffee."

There's something going on here. Major Fulvio Cantini is a fine actor. His voice is authentic, almost like a Renaissance painting. Has A. sought out my father to lessen his sense of guilt? I don't believe so. Just as I don't believe A. has told him the truth. If he had given him the same story he gave to me, Andrea Berti would be a dead man. I put off further questions for a later date and tell my father good bye in a distracted way, pretending that another call is coming in.

I spend the rest of the afternoon with my pots and stove like a good housewife. I take the plastic apron, which I've only used a few times, from the hook on the kitchen wall. Lucio Spasimo will have to be satisfied with mashed potatoes, a store-bought mousse, and two filets of sole that I've kept wrapped in plastic in the freezer for who knows how long.

Precisely at eight, the slayer of internet pirates arrives with a bottle of Chianti and a bouquet of different colored buttercups. He wears a light pink V-neck pullover, a black jacket, and baggy trousers that make him look slender. He must have gone home to change clothes. He's amazed to see that I've set the table with a clean tablecloth, nice plates, coasters for the bottles, and candles, which I move aside to make room for a flower vase. Chaos reigns in the unartistic rest of the house, but the kitchen is warm and welcoming.

As I fill the plates, Spasimo coughs: "The professor phoned twice after you left."

"How did he sound?" I remark with feigned indifference.

"He sounded like someone who's looking for you because he has something to tell you."

"He's already said what he has to tell me."

We sit at the table. I light a cigarette and blow smoke in his face. He, with his knife in midair and the sole in his plate, cracks a joke. "Excuse me, but does it bother you if I eat while you smoke?"

"No, no, go right ahead…"

Half-way through the meal, tired of putting it off, I give him the recent news. Spasimo listens to me, filling my glass now and then.

"Giorgia, it's nobody's fault," he says at last.

"For Andrea Berti," I reply sharply, "Ada was just a girl who would sell herself to the first pimp she met on her way to becoming rich and famous."

He doesn't bat an eye.

I look at him. "Lucio, have you ever been in love?"

"One time I thought I was. He arranged to meet me in front of Teatro Rialto, but he never showed up. A few days later, I learned he was going to get married."

"Let's forget about it then."

"You know how men are… If you treat them badly, they fall in love."

I watch him jab at the potatoes with his fork. "You don't like it?"

"I'm sure you acted in good faith."

"What do you mean?"

"That you didn't intend to poison me… Ah, Frank also called today. He wanted to say goodbye before he left. He's going on tour with Tenga, Venga…"

"Renga. Francesco Renga."

"You know him?"

"You ought to get a radio and listen to it while you work."

"I will one day. The mousse?"

"It's chilling."

He leans toward me and clears his voice. "What do you think it matters to Ada if you've met her Andrea Berti, who is no longer that Andrea Berti, but an Andrea Berti with an extra twenty years on his back?"

I push my plate away. "A somewhat superficial analysis, don't you think?"

"Men don't know how to deal with emotions. They're big fuckups. They make a mess of things…"

Luckily, Tim has been giving me weed for the past few months. While Spasimo eats his mousse, which I've coated with an entire can of whipped cream, I roll a joint in silence. After a while, the thick smell of marijuana starts to dissipate.

Spasimo removes his glasses and places them on the table. I feel his myopic, bulging eyes observing me. "Is that her?" he asks, pointing to a framed photo of Ada on a shelf.

I nod yes.

"You're full of rage now. And you can't stand it that an egocentric twenty-year old, who used to snort coke and drink like a fish, saw your sister swinging from…"

"It wasn't a swing, Lucio!"

He smacks his hands on the table cloth. "Let me finish."

"Then use different words."

I pass him the joint, but he makes a sign of refusal. "Both of them had changed, Giorgia. Ada wasn't herself. It's strange you really don't understand…"

I twist the muscles of my face into a grimace. "He didn't stop her."

"How many people say they're going to kill themselves and then don't follow through…"

My nerves are jumping. "Whose side are you on anyway?"

"Yours. But you're crucifying this Andrea Berti."

"Women and elephants never forget, Spasimo. Dorothy Parker said so."

"Oh, you always need an enemy. You go from your father to…"

"I barely restrain myself. "What's my father got to do with it?"

"Don't you think your father suffers because of what happened? Does his life seem like a life to you"?

"And what is it?"

"Your father hits the bottle so you won't have to deal with this situation by yourself."

I spring up from my chair and begin to make coffee. "Do me the favor…"

"Look at her," he points to the photo of Ada. "You can't talk to her. You can't touch her, because that's the problem: You're alive and she's not. It's a case that can't be solved."

"What are you trying to tell me? That life goes on? Spasimo, no crap like that from you…"

"It's egotistic, Giorgia, to think that grief is a condition that doesn't change. Your ego won't let you move forward. Yes, you've said it well. Life goes on."

I lean against the glass front of the armoire. "My blood recoils at the thought that his hands…"

"I have to tell you: I feel sorry for every man who gets close to you."

"Why?"

He leans his head to one side. "Well, you seem so self-sufficient. That is, you do everything you can so people will think that."

I sit back down at the table and light a Camel. "I'll explain something to you, Spasimo. One day they call the house, and you answer the phone. A kind voice has difficulty finding the words to tell you that your sister has strangled herself with the strap of her purse. You shut yourself up in your room, and you rail against the fate that ripped her away from you like a limb. You feel mutilated, exactly so, mutilated. But then time passes. Even if you always have a red eye, you find a reason for it, you see? Shit, it never heals…"

The coffee gurgles in the espresso maker. I get up and pour it into cups. "Our house was full of people. Everyone telling me what to do, everyone with his own medicine, his own plan, my aunt, my father's colleagues, even the grocer."

"And you?"

"I looked at my father sitting in a corner, upset, desperate," I say waving my arms.

Spasimo grabs hold of my sweater. "And you?"

I see a coffee stain spreading on the table cloth.

"Giorgia," he says without relaxing his grip, "where is it written that we have to be strong?"

At midnight, when Spasimo gets out of my car, a few pounds heavier and fearful of having said something to offend me, I reassure him with an awkward kiss on the cheek. I have no desire to ask myself if the things he's said to me are true or not. The only thing I know for certain is that just thinking about Andrea Berti makes me want to throw up.

I find an open pharmacy and a sleepy doctor, who sells me a small bottle of eye drops. "Three drops, twice a day," he advises me.

Later, when I enter the Osteria delle Mura, Gigi Marini is reading an article in *La Repubblica* on "smart" bombs.

"Hey," I greet him and then turn to the girl who's waiting on tables: "A medium light beer."

"I was really moved by your telephone call," he says ironically while folding the paper.

I stretch my arms lazily on the table surface. "If only all my days were like this, medium light."

"And how are they instead?"

"Dark. Very dark."

"Your face is…"

"I haven't slept for two nights." I watch him slide his wedding ring off and on. "Your wife never gets pissed off?"

He shrugs his shoulders. "She's the wife of a musician."

I sip my beer. "Indeed."

I go to the newspaper and unfold it. No article about the investigation of Donatella Verze. Perhaps she'll become a popular topic again the day they discover her killer, then she'll be completely forgotten.

"So," he says drumming his fingers on the table, "why did you call me?"

"Because your cell phone is always on."

"Right. Certainly not for a quickie, seeing what you said to me the last time."

"What did I say?"

He lowers his voice. "That you never come."

"Almost never," I correct him.

"Even worse." His laughter sounds like a sob. "And how are things going with the young kid?"

"What kid?"

"The one I always see you going around with. It's fashionable among forty-year old women, isn't it?"

My laughter breaks him up.

"You mean, you're not sleeping with him?"

"Gigi, I leave this stupid fucking around with twenty-year olds completely to you guys."

"Look, I've never liked young girls."

I look at him. "Explain something to me. Why do you fuck me? Certainly not for the physical pleasure."

He lights a Pall Mall. "You always underrate yourself, Giorgia."

It's three in the morning, and Gigi and I collapse on the bed of a cheap, anonymous room in the Astor Pensione. Once again, his wife will force herself to believe that he lost track of things at the end of a jam session, staying up late drinking beer in some dive.

As soon as he opens my wind breaker and slips a hand under my top, I realize that having or not having sex with him is really the same thing. The indifference in my eyes puts him off, and for a while I'm looking elsewhere beyond this room, just like my mother and sister.

"Do you want to turn out the light?"

"I want you to go home."

Gigi Marini leaves the bed and starts striding up and down the room. "You're very strange."

I cross my legs on the bed, blink my eyelids, and nod.

"OK, I'm off. What will you do?"

I shake the bottle of eye drops. "You've already paid for the room."

When I hear the door shut, I concentrate on putting the drops in my right pupil.

Tell me that it wasn't a joke, Ada. Tell me that you thought about it and that it wasn't just the delirium of a girl who loses control, as in that song by Joy Division. Tell me that the pain was too much and that it had to be stopped, in whatever way, at whatever cost, because you had this cursed right — we all have it — to throw away your life like a heavy coat, which made you sweat, which you had to remove to feel light and say to yourself: 'Hurray, I've done it, I don't feel anything anymore, I'm not hot or cold, I don't love and I don't hate, I'm dead, I'm safe, take care of yourselves, I'm fine, now it's up to you to speak the next lines!'

I close my eyes.

"You'll get wet," I tell her, "and you'll catch cold."

She shrugged, continuing to stretch her arms out the window. We were in our room at the beach house, in Lido di Savio, and we heard Papa having a discussion with Aunt Lidia in the next room. It was the first summer without Mama, and the insupportable gloom of those days had unleashed a storm full of lightning bolts, almost cartoon-like. Far away, you could glimpse the turbulent sea, and Ada imagined the phosphorescent tails of eels and crabs overturned in the sand.

"Move back," I said, drawing her by the rain-soaked sleeve of her night shirt. She pushed me away. A man, in the villa facing us, had edged aside the window curtain and was staring at her. Ada, with a crooked smile and the eyes of a lost soul, slipped off her night shirt and pointed her breasts against the glass window. The man, with his pants lowered, began to move his cock in her direction.

CHAPTER 15

Sitting in my office on the leather armchair is the engineer, Guido Comolli, just returned from Switzerland. He's about five-eleven, thin and pale like one of the slim cigarettes his daughter smokes. After a quick handshake, he sits back down, and I open a desk drawer and remove a brown leather folder containing the photos of Mrs. Comolli and her lover.

Gaia's father examines the photos with morbid attention, narrowing his small watery eyes and emitting a cynical laugh from time to time. "In Boccaccio's *Decameron*, Messer Rossiglione makes his wife eat the heart of her lover." With that, he takes a checkbook from his briefcase and signs one of them. I'm more concerned about Gaia than I am about his wife or her lover.

"What will you do now?" I ask.

Perhaps he despises me for my naivety. "I'll talk to my lawyers."

"And your daughter?"

"My daughter? You should see her, she eats almost nothing. Her psychotherapist does what she can. After Simone died of meningitis, she's never been the same."

Maybe I didn't hear correctly. "I'm sorry, what did you say?"

"A family matter." He rises from the chair with an elegant motion and shakes my hand. "Congratulations, you've done good work."

As soon as Comolli leaves, I call Tim on the phone.

"Is Gaia with you?"

"No, I'm seeing her later. I'm on my way to the department. By the way, Berti asked about you yesterday."

I pretend I didn't hear him. "Where can I find her?"

"At home… I don't know. Why?"

"Nothing, nothing."

138

I'm about to say something else. "Look, boss, I'm not stringing her along."

There's a lump in my throat. I still haven't read her poems. I don't think I'm someone who reads poetry.

When I ring the doorbell at the Comolli's house, Adam, their boxer, starts barking at me until the maid comes and grabs hold of him. He's not a scary dog, but you never know. Gaia pops up from behind the house with a plant in her hand. "Taking up gardening?" I ask her.

She rests the plant on the ground and wipes her dirty hands against the fabric of her jeans. "You know, I'm thinking of studying literature at the university."

"It's a great idea."

There's a moment of embarrassment. Gaia didn't expect to see me, and I didn't expect to come here.

"I wanted to ask you if you'd like to come with me."

"Where?"

I pass my hand through my hair and don't answer.

"Give me a minute," she says.

I see her climb the steps and disappear inside the house. I hear her mother reminding her to come back for lunch. It will be a different lunch from the usual, I think. Perhaps the engineer will scatter my photos between the porcelain tureens and the silver napkin rings.

For the entire trip to the Certosa Cemetery, Gaia and I say nothing to each other. I park, we get out of the Citroën, and we walk up to the entrance way.

Here it is, enormous and silent, the place where Charon ferries the souls of the city to the other bank. Long ago, someone described it as the most cheerful place in Bologna: "City of porticos that hide the light, with its Two Towers, leaning in different directions, giving you vertigo…"

Gaia is calm like a trusty sidekick. "Do you want to take some flowers?" she asks me.

"Later," I say. "Now show me where Simone is."

She starts back, ready to flee.

"No, wait," I block her way. "I know why you always come here."

She breathes heavily as she darts by me with a fierce, defiant glance.

"Calm down," I tell her. "I just want to see him."

In the photo panel, Simone Comolli is a chubby baby wearing a red outfit and a sports cap.

"Why didn't you tell me about him?" I ask her.

She coughs as if from a nervous reaction. "I enjoy having some secrets," she answers me firmly. Then as we walk in the direction of Ada's grave: "I was the one who looked after him. My father, with all his money, wasn't able to save him. It's nice when someone depends on you. He was always following me, the two of us in that big house you could get lost in. I hated him when he fell sick, I really did. I was mad at him. My parents explained nothing to me. According to them, things were clearly starting to get worse. No one discussed it. Maybe that's why I started writing…"

She takes a deep breath and continues: "I loved my brother. I still do. I come here and talk to him. I know he doesn't hear me. I know there are too many dead because there isn't a place large enough for all of them…but there has to be some sort of contact, right? If there isn't, if death is sleep, I tell myself: "When he died, Simone knew it. He knew that I loved him."

"I'm certain he knew it," I reassure her.

"Even if I ran away? Even if I wasn't there?"

"Did he die in the hospital?"

"Yes."

I light up a Camel. "I swear to God, he knew it."

"You don't believe in God."

I look around. In my eyes, grave stones upon grave stones, marble or iron crosses, vaults, slabs…

Gaia crushes a Philip Morris under one of her white Adidas sneakers.

"Your mother?" she asks me.

I shrug my shoulders. "She isn't here."

She nods at the photo of Ada. "People say that…well, essentially, it's a hereditary condition?"

I rub my right eye with my hand. "I hope not."

As I turn around and walk toward the cemetery exit, I hear her say: "If I were to lose you, I couldn't take it."

It's hard to look at her right now.

I'd like to tell her that it won't happen and that I expect the same thing from her: not to go away, not to vanish from my life. But I take her back home without saying a word.

An hour later, I hear the doorbell ring while I'm changing clothes. I stumble toward the door, hitching up my pants as best I can. When I open it, I see Andrea Berti and start to shut it, but he quickly slips a foot inside the doorway.

"What do you want?"

"To talk."

"And that?" I ask, pointing to the bottle of Pinot.

"It's for me. May I open it?"

I let him inside, I show him the kitchen, and I watch him search for a corkscrew in the drawers of a cabinet. At last he finds it and a glass too, and pours himself some wine. "Do you want some?"

I open the fridge and take out a container of yogurt and cereal. "No."

He sits on the sofa and moves aside a pair of slippers and an undershirt. "I meant to give you more time — enough time to think about things calmly. But I haven't succeeded."

"I see."

As I dig my tiny spoon into the yogurt, I feel his blue eyes inside me like a danger I've escaped. ("I've slept with wild beasts," goes a song by Tom Waits.)

I watch him take another sip and then pass his tongue over his teeth. "I wanted to tell you that I never thought about Ada while we were together. Maybe because you're not like her. Maybe because I never understood anything about her."

I lean against the door that separates the living room from the kitchen, and I have no intention of sitting down. "Are you finished?"

"I'd just prefer that you don't judge me."

I pronounce the letters emphatically. "FOR-GET-ABOUT-IT."

"Patty, the girl at the pet store, told me that you've been inquiring about me."

I toss the container in the trash. "Old story."

"One time Ada spoke to me about you. She considered you a hard nut, and said you'd become a great lawyer. Perhaps that's why she didn't confide in you. She was afraid of disillusioning you..."

I've bought the pregnancy test at the pharmacy. You'd have to be completely crazy to bring someone into the world...

"Was she pregnant?"

He gets up off the sofa, and we stare at each other for a few seconds. And he's the one who finally looks away. "I don't know why I've come to see you."

"Me neither."

He heads quickly toward the door.

I raise my voice. "What's your connection to my father?"

"Ask him."

I hear the sound of the door shutting. Given the circumstances, Andrea Berti and I will never end up like the people you see in advertisements. We won't wake up and have breakfast together in a custom-designed Scavolini kitchen with bowls of cornflakes in front of us.

I throw myself on the bed in the dark. The street lights are reflected in the photo of Ada on the bedside table. I wonder what she would have become if she were here now. An actress? A writer? Someone's wife?

A dead person doesn't wonder who she could have been, who she would have become, whether a success or a failure. This is something I ask myself, I who am alive enough to be forty-years old next July. Did I ever have dreams? Dreams perhaps of changing the world when I took part in student demonstrations or picketed in front of the high school during strike days. I never dreamed of becoming a musician, for example. All I wanted was to bang the drums loudly to deafen the buzzing noise I heard in my head. It wasn't the artistry that drew me toward the tom-tom, the cymbals, or the snare. Mine was an all-out thrashing to discharge my nerves. For some people it's fighting, for others it's the workout, for me it was the drums.

No one urged me to become a lawyer. And love, well, it was the same as a trip to the zoo — something to watch from behind locked windows or doors. I don't do this work by chance. I see wild animals tear each other apart, I photograph them, I document them, I archive them… What's the phrase I hear repeated most often? Here it is: "I was faithful." Show them the evidence of adultery, and you'll hear them say: "He betrayed my trust." Then you'd like to ask: "What the hell is trust? Why do all of you have this word on your lips?" To rely on yourself is already a difficult task, to expect it of others is craziness! I don't believe people who never go off track, and I don't want heroes at my feet. I don't rub my clean conscience in someone's face and then scold him for having trampled in shit. I don't have a clean conscience! Fine. So…why did I treat Andrea Berti this way?

It's been years since Ada and I told each other something about our day (before going to sleep and listening in the dark to songs like "To Feel in Love" by Lucio Battisti or "Little Man" by Mia Martini).

At fourteen, in front of Liceo Galvani, I forced passersby to answer questions about the new child-labor law, and I hated the little fascists who sat on the steps making fun of me. During the day, I studied Thomas Aquinas, and at night I went to the movies to see films like *Salt of the Earth* by Herbert Biberman.

One summer for my birthday, Papa took us to the Arena in Verona to see *Aida*, and while Ada was moved by the opera and the singers, I felt passion only during the two minutes of silence to commemorate the Jews who died in the Ardeatine Massacre and to protest against the flight of Kappler. In those years, I was only interested in studying ancient philosophers, talking about war with Iranian friends, making pamphlets in the department, hanging up posters for a Unity Festival, peeling potatoes in a kitchen stall, and following debates on anti-fascism. All things that Ada did not understand or believed I did just to irritate Papa, since I was his little darling in every other way.

The only boy I hung out with was Fabio. He took part in the student movement and strummed the guitar. Aside from discussing politics on the number 10 bus or exchanging the album *Roots* by Francesco Guccini, we never gave each other a single kiss. I spoke to him about Marx or nuclear energy and quoted from *The Words to Say It*, a novel by Marie Cardinal, even though now and then he would have preferred talking about other stuff. One day he said to me: "I feel old. Why can't I have fun at a disco?"

We were sitting in the living room of his house and watching the Sanremo Music Festival with Roberto Benigni. "Discos are places for idiots," I told him. And meanwhile I thought of my sister, who came home at two in the morning from the Ciak, sweaty and tipsy after dancing for hours, ready to take the customary two slaps from my father without batting an eyelid and without stopping, not even for a second, from smiling as if that vague and vacant smile was her secret weapon against the world.

Andrea Berti left this house half an hour ago. How absurd to think that he's the one, right now, to whom I'd like to explain how much or little I know about my sister.

We would come home from the theatre, Ada and I. She'd take off her coat. So would I, and in the same way. By imitating her, I believed I was playing it safe.

When she turned off the night-light over the bed-side table, I would ask her: "Ada, but what is love?" Because if someone had asked me what a notebook was or a tree or a radiator, I would have known how to respond, but I knew nothing about that particular thing — love.

"It's like going out to sea in a boat with someone and then wanting to go back."

"To the shore?"

"Yes, to the shore."

I flicked my eyes in the dark, trying to grasp the sense of her metaphor. It's only now I understand that for her this shore-offshore was her solitude, loved and hated, pushed aside but always there, in sight, like something you keep in the corner of your eye throughout your life.

I tossed and turned in bed, thinking that one day, when I really wanted it, I'd fall in love with a fresh-water sailor, kind and considerate, or with an Olympic athlete or a philosopher.

"For Empedocles," I told her, "every similar thing seeks its own likeness."

And she: "For Heraclitus, harmony springs from opposites."

Then I folded the pillow in two and propped myself on my elbow. "Ada, do you know where I can find some digitalis?"

"What is it?"

"A plant," I answered, not mentioning that I had just read in a book by Stendhal that digitalis is a plant that keeps the heart from beating too strongly. A plant that I wanted to administer to her every time she returned home infatuated and full of exaggerated emotion for some boy at school.

"Do you really want to ask Papa to buy you a drum-set?"

"Of course."

"He'll never do it."

"Then I'll play someone else's."

(And so it happened, in Mel's sound-proof basement on Via Crocetta, and it was a green Pearl drum-set that had belonged to his brother before he took up the guitar.)

"And you'll go to Rome?"

"If it's the last thing I do in my life," she said with utter confidence.

"I'll miss," I whispered, "not hearing you play 'The Turkish March' any more."

CHAPTER 16

When I enter the agency, I see Tim displaying the latest peace flag outside the window. He has already prepared his backpack for the trip to Rome to march against the war, and Gaia will naturally go with him. I observe them speaking softly, their mouths close to each other, without hiding anything, without using the cryptic language of grown-ups, full of double meanings and allusions. She's in the process of moving. She'll go to live with her mother and the colleague of her father, who has left his wife and is staying in a hotel for now. I give them a farewell hug, and as I shut myself in the office, I hear Spasimo advising Tim to stay out of trouble.

I'm standing in front of the office window. I have on my woolen turtle-neck sweater, with my hands on the radiator, and yet I still feel cold. With my nose an inch from the glass pane, I see a man striding confidently on the sidewalk. He vaguely resembles an actor whose name I don't remember. Oh, yeah, George Clooney. Instead, it's Alessandro Dazi.

At that moment, the phone on the desk starts ringing. I pick up the receiver and say "hello" three times. Nothing, absolute silence. I hang up.

Dazi looks dazzling — freshly shaven and sporting an Armani suit with a purple-and-green-striped silk tie. "I'm here because I have a debt to settle with you."

"Of course."

He lights a Davidoff. "May I confide in you?" He doesn't wait for an answer. "My ex-wife wants to remarry, and I feel bad about it. It's hard to accept that a woman you've been with can belong to someone else."

"Do you still love her?"

"Tonight I screwed a Nigerian girl."

"Ah," I say, pressing up against the back of the swivel chair.

"I was at a dinner full of beautiful women, and there were a few I could easily have gone to bed with."

"I imagine so."

"Courting women is hard work."

"Better a Nigerian."

He laughs faintly, showing off his perfect teeth. "I've walked away from the lives of many women, who are still wondering why."

"Are you proud of it?"

"Certainly not."

I watch him with polite indifference, waiting for him to hurry up and say what he wants to say.

"My ex-wife and I quarreled constantly."

I light a cigarette. "Then you were smart to get a divorce."

"Your sister was an actress?"

I nod through long puffs of smoke.

"Angela used to organize so many parties. Actors and singers came to them... Who knows, I may have met her."

I rub my tired and swollen eyes. If it were summer, I'd turn on the fan and aim it right at his face, hoping to see him fly away, light as a leaf, out the door.

"How much do I owe you?" he asks me.

"Only the money for the train ticket."

"Is that enough?"

"Yes, that's enough."

He takes a pair of bank notes from his wallet and places them on the table. "I believe I've already asked you, but I'll try again. I'd like to invite you to dinner — out of friendship."

I feel as heavy as a housewife who has lugged her grocery bags up five flights of stairs. "Yes, of course, Dazi, please call me sometime."

I see him smile with a note of satisfaction. "You're different from all the women I've met."

"How so?"

"You don't even seem like a woman."

I'm curious. "Because a woman is like what?"

"What I mean is that I like talking to you, while in general I only seek out women to sleep with them."

I walk with him to the door. "I'm a little hurt that you don't want to sleep with me."

He promptly says: "Can I do something about that?"

Alessandro Dazi has been gone for a few minutes when I hear someone knocking at the door.

"What is it?"

Spasimo stands there leaning against the door frame. "How did it go?"

"It will please you to know that I just accepted an invitation to dinner from Dazi."

"I don't believe it."

"Are you jealous?"

He leaves, acting the part of the betrayed lover. It's great to hear our laughter going from one room to another.

The phone rings again. It's Mel. "So how did it go in Monaco?" I ask him.

"She took me ice skating on a pond."

"Oh," I tease him, "it seems like a serious relationship."

"How could it be? It's a long-distance relationship."

"What's the problem? You're always moving... Why don't you just relocate there?"

(Maybe he's already thought about it.) "You know, I even tried to convince myself to visit a Brazilian fortune teller who reads sea shells."

I laugh. "What did the sea shells say?"

"A lot of bullshit. It's not easy to start a new relationship at forty. But we're lucky, we have music. *Music is your only friend until the end...*"

"Who said that?"

"Jim Morrison."

I say goodbye to him with a promise that we'll see each other soon.

I start reading my email, and I find a message from Aldo. I dial the number of his house in Willesdone Road, and he responds on the first ring.

"It's good to hear from you," he says to me.

"How's it going?"

"Everything's the same except that I've met a really sweet girl, who teaches at Middlesex Polytechnic... And she's married. And you?"

"Same as always."

We stay silent, both of us thinking the same thing, that it's better not to talk about Ada.

"Giorgia, why don't you come visit me?"

Oh yeah, it's been a lifetime since I toured that city where cigarettes cost a fortune. I'd like to say yes, but I feel like the time that Mel and I spent going from one music store to another in Charing Cross is too far in the past.

"I'll think about it," I say.

I say good bye, sending him a kiss and wishing him the best of luck with the married teacher.

I return home, and I'm not hungry. Thirty cigarettes have already filled my stomach. I call Gigi Martini on his cell phone, but he doesn't answer, and I ask myself what his motive is for wanting to spend time with me. He's used to getting signals from attractive women in their thirties, sitting at night-club tables, fascinated by his pyrotechnic fingers on the keyboard and his tortured look. I imagine him holding his drink and sitting down to tell his story of the time he had the honor of meeting Michel Petrucciani. Women are drawn to his bad-boy aura, and so let themselves be driven around in a car that reeks of cigarettes and spilled beer under the seats, carpeted with truck stop receipts. They don't realize he's a jazz musician. If you've given him some affection, he can go along with you, but then he finishes the night reeling through the streets with a dog behind him and the rain in his face, destructively in love with his own shadow silhouetted on a wall. What did he say to me the first time I met him? "O jazz, those gentlemen and convicts with fiery souls. The class of Kenny Clarke, the stormy rhythms of Elvin Jones, the sweat of Satchmo, the sweetness of Chet, the fights of Mingus, the voice of Billy…" Ah, we were both really drunk.

I could call Dazi, but I have no wish to listen to a masochistic ego-trip with a lobster in front of me. I phone Lucio.

"Still in the office?"

"Yes, but I'm leaving."

I don't manage to hide my disappointment. "Too bad."

"Problems?"

"I'm fine. Where are you going?"

"To the movies."

"Alone?"

Silence at the other end.

"Sorry I asked," and I'm about to hang up.

"Giorgia, are you there?"

"By Jove." (Strange, I never say "by Jove.")

"His name is Josh. He's from Sacramento. An IT guy."

(Yet more proof that I don't pay attention. I see Spasimo every day. And what do I know about him?)

After an eternity, I answer. "The blue pullover, the one with the horizontal gray stripe across the chest. It looks fantastic on you."

Maybe he's laughing. "Ah, Giorgia. Bruni called. He says it's important."

I open a Bud and look at the shoe box at the foot of the sofa.

No trace of my sister's artistry remains, not a video, not a scene photo, nothing, only my memory of her shouting in front of our bedroom mirror: "Don't turn on the light!" And she was the best Blanche DuBois that I've ever seen.

January 31, 1986

Dear Aldo,

It was wonderful staying up late talking to you about a novel that you haven't yet written, but whose title you already have in mind. I rushed back from Bologna because a screen test in Rome was waiting for me, which I did not pass. I wonder how long I'll manage to last in this world where you only land a part if you slobber like a dog on the pants of the master. The theatre was my utopia, and I wanted it to open up for me like a window. I was prepared to welcome everything: sounds, words, newspaper pages, used tampons, wild flowers. I wanted to express all these things in order to please people, to make them laugh or cry, and not receive bouquets of roses in a dressing room or end up in bed with some politician. Now I've tried everything, and I'm tired of "live" acting because they won't allow me in the designated places. I envy Giorgia, who has a different personality and different aspirations, and sometimes I hate my mother for all those heart-breaking French songs she made me listen to as a little girl. I find it revolting to lick someone's hands for a crumb of attention. Just as I can't stand the lukewarm devotion of Giulio, his paternal concern, and I think that only with A., in his bed of nettles, do I succeed in feeling evanescent or fleeting, as you'd say. I'm not foolish enough to think that he's in love with me — my capacity for self-delusion hasn't reached that point, but at least with him I can drink and pull out the thorn…

I'm jolted by the ringing of my cordless phone, half-hidden on the glass table by a flesh-colored stocking. I lift the receiver up lazily. On the other end: rasping and muttering.

"I thought of you today," says my Aunt Lidia in the tone of someone who generally thinks about things more important than me.

"How so?" I say through a veil of irony.

"I ran into a college friend of yours, Chiara something, at the supermarket."

"Chiara Vanni?"

"Yes, that's her. She's a little plump, but she's still a beauty."

"Is that so?"

"Yes, despite four pregnancies."

"Then it's normal she should have put on a few pounds."

"The same thing is true for you, but without children for an excuse."

I'd like to thank her for the subtle reminder, but I let it go. "The word 'friend' is too much. We saw each other just to study together, to prepare for tests, to exchange notes…"

(Chiara Vanni, unlike me, managed to finish university. But I suppose she never took advantage of her law degree. Four children are a demanding enough job.)

"Am I mistaken or did you often sleep at her house?"

"She lived far away, and Papa wasn't always able to come and fetch me."

I see the hairs standing on my arms, and I turn cold because I already know what Aunt Lidia is about to say.

"Even the night your sister died."

The walls of Chiara Vanni's bedroom were painted pink, and she had a collection of hideous stuffed animals — presents from her boyfriends — in a Barbie-style chest of drawers. I gave her a David Bowie poster (dressed in coat and tails) and another poster of a Paul Klee painting, but she never hung them up.

That night, Papa telephoned and told Chiara's father that he had car problems. He would have it towed to the garage in the morning. Could they put me up for the night?

My aunt is talking about something, and I interrupt her brusquely. "Aunt Lidia, try to focus," I tell her.

She mumbles in agreement.

"Say what you remember," I explain.

I hear her breathe, waiting.

"The night that Ada died, I was at the Vanni's house. I came back home the following morning. Papa was at work…"

"Yes, yes, I remember."

"I thought…Papa's car broke down…"

"Oh, that piece of junk was always breaking down. Chiara Vanni, however, told me to give you her best. She feels bad that you haven't married and still don't have children…"

I interrupt her again. "Did you have dinner with Papa that night?"

"You know, I always ate dinner at your house ever since… What a shame," she sighs. "It was such a nice house. I told Fulvio he shouldn't sell it."

I relax against the sofa. "How are the cats?"

"Fine, fine…but not that night. I telephoned your father that night, but he wasn't there. I was really worried, and I called him again at midnight. Nothing. The next day I asked him where he ended up. He used to drink from time to time, you know…"

"And what was his answer?"

"They had just called from Rome. There were other things to think about at that moment," she cuts me short.

CHAPTER 17

I park the Citroën in front of a sooty brick building and think about my father. At this hour, he's no doubt eating dinner in front of the TV. I pass through the wrought-iron gate. I look at the orderly hedges and an old woman shaking out a table cloth at the window. Soon my father, in sandals and woolen bathrobe, opens the door. He doesn't seem happy to see me, and I was expecting it.

From our old house he's brought to this place only some antique furniture and the library. I glance at the piles of books that suffocate the thirty square-foot room, and it brings to mind Dylan Thomas, who said that a library is a clinic of mental illnesses. Without saying a word to me, he goes into the kitchen to finish washing the dishes, and I follow him.

After a while he asks, "Would you like some barley coffee?"

I indicate yes and sit down at a square table with a silver tray in the middle, while he opens the door of a cupboard painted mint-green and takes out a jar of coffee. I look away from the row of Anisette bottles on the cabinet and watch the fake smile of a TV presenter, as he interviews some supposed experts on the Cogne murder case. I pluck up courage and place the shoe box I've brought with me on the table. "Papa," I say, "these are Ada's letters. Do you want to read them?"

My father throws the soapy sponge into the drainer, goes to the TV, and changes the channel. On a talk show, someone is discussing the war against Iraq; I see my father nod at the news that North Korea is building a bomb. I realize too late that a provoking remark is about to escape my mouth. "Well, you're right after all. The Americans' suicide is more important than my sister's…"

The Major seizes a rag he uses to dry the dishes and heads for a photo sitting in its glass frame on a shelf in the cupboard.

I watch him dust off, delicately and meticulously, the faces of my mother, my sister, and me. There is Mrs. Ilaria Cantini, nee Maggi, lying in a meadow in a cream-colored suit. She smiles at Ada and me doing somersaults in front of the camera.

As I watch my father perform this gesture, I wonder if he and I will ever talk about the subject of our family. But perhaps there are gestures that say everything. Perhaps nothing is more explicit than his hand that caresses the glass. Then, I think, it's not like a movie where one person goes up to another and says, "Just cry on my shoulder," and everyone thinks, "Finally, it all comes out." In life, it doesn't always happen like that. In life, there is some weeping that can't be allowed or that can't be induced without also taking someone down, all the way down.

My father pours my coffee into a large blue cup, chipped at the edge — another thing that came with him during the move and that forms part of the old tea service. He pours himself some Anisette and takes off his glasses to blur his view of the old photo behind me.

I can't restrain myself. "Where were you the night Ada killed herself?"

The glass of Anisette slips from his hand and shatters on the floor. Instinctively, I start to bend down, but my father is quicker. He gets up, grabs a dust pan, gathers the pieces of glass, and tosses them in the trash bin. Then he sits at the table again, arms crossed, and stares at the wall.

"As always, I was at home."

"I spoke to Aunt Lidia... I'm tired, Papa."

He nods and sighs. "You slept at Chiara Vanni's house that night, remember? Your friend from college... It was very late when I got to Rome. I wanted to see clearly what your sister was up to. She opened the door in a black undershirt, with a half-empty bottle of whiskey in her hand. I went inside and saw a boy sprawled on the sofa. He was rubbing his gums. I asked her if she had been drinking, and she laughed in my face. I couldn't stand it. When I ordered her to get dressed and told her I was taking her away, she started yelling and insulting me. The boy said he was leaving so we could talk by ourselves, and he left. It all happened so fast, Giorgia. You have no idea how fast some things happen. I went into the bathroom to wash my face, and then sat on the edge of the tub to think. Ada had just told me that it was all my fault if Mama…"

I pour some Anisette in my cup.

"Your mother was always in a bad mood. She had her pills, a lover, and a carabiniere for a husband. She always said it with loathing: "carabiniere." Slowly, slowly we grew apart. It happens like that in certain marriages. And when she decided to crush herself in the car against the gate, I was full of resentment. I thought: "What do I know about this woman?""

He gets up, takes another glass, and fills it to the brim with Anisette.

"I left the bathroom, and Ada was there, on her feet, drinking straight from the bottle. It seemed like a script from one of her… You know how she was, don't you?"

My voice is a whisper. "No, Papa, I don't know how she was. I don't know."

I go out to buy Vermouth wearing a raincoat over my pajamas, with dirty hair and bags under my eyes like someone who's had a long night of sex. When I return, I find a book by Colette and another one by Anaïs Nin waiting for me on the bedside table, but I turn on the TV and watch The Searchers *at full volume. Giulio is fed up, he says he can't handle seeing me depressed, and then he asks where I've spent the night…*

"I put my hands over my ears to keep from hearing her."

"Why?"

"She was laughing. She never stopped laughing."

I tell him that I miss my piano. That it's going out of tune at home and filling up with dust…

"I opened the door to the apartment and ran away."

But it's not just the piano that I miss, Aldo. I also miss our snow-sledding, the juke-box tokens, "Give Me a Smile" by Drupi, your blue Citroën Dyane, the way Giorgia smelled when she was nine: ditto for Doriano crackers…

"She was alive. When I left her, Ada was alive. After the funeral, I looked for that boy everywhere, but he had vanished into thin air. And then the other day he called me, and we met."

"I know that. What did he want?"

I see the sideways movement of his head and his lips curled into a half smile. "When he came back that night, Andrea Berti found the door ajar. I must have left it like that. He went inside, and Ada was already dead. For all these years, he's believed I was somehow involved, and I thought it was his fault…that he had come back…they had a fight. Instead, Ada died between my leaving and his return. In the twelve minutes when she was alone."

And then I miss my mother…

His hand trembles as he grips the glass. "Neither one of us was present…"

(No witness. No failure to stop and give help. Isn't that what they'd say in a TV movie?)

"But what does that change? There is always plenty you can blame yourself for. He was just a mixed-up kid, and I always made mistakes with your sister. Perhaps I failed the entire family, and the best part of me I gave away to strangers."

"Why didn't Andrea tell me his suspicions about you?"

"Because he wanted to protect you."

My father gulps down his Anisette, and I pick up my shoebox. We both rise at the same time. I head for the door. He goes to the TV and turns up the volume.

CHAPTER 18

It's been a quiet morning in the agency: a few phone calls, some checks cashed, and a woman who hasn't heard from her son (living in Paris) for two months and doesn't know whether to turn to the Italian Consulate or to the TV show *Chi l'ha visto?* Even Germana Bonini has stopped by, happy as a clam for the return of her husband: apparently, the dancer from Bolzano has gone abroad with a choreographer.

After lunch, a woman showed up: mid-forties, tall and slender, low forehead, unruly red curls, black and vacant eyes. She wore a fox coat over a tight-fitting dress that accentuated her tiny breasts. For the first fifteen minutes, she was very laconic and answered my questions with a nod of yes or no. When she felt more at ease, she told me about her husband (a businessman fearful of bankruptcy) and about his nights spent away from home with who-the-hell-knows.

"My husband says I'm too emotional and live through my imagination…" After dropping her arms to her sides, she concluded in a choked up voice: "I'm here to discover the truth."

"Do you love him?" I asked her.

She put her head between her hands and rolled her eyes. "Look, I can't imagine living without him for very long."

"Then why do you care about knowing the truth?"

Open-mouthed, she stared me in the eyes.

"Don't be in a rush," I continued and strode with long, firm steps towards the door. "Wait a few days. I'm always here, if you need me. Call whenever you like."

"But I…"

"Now please go."

She tossed her head back, looking at the ceiling, then she rose from the arm chair. I followed her to the door, watched her walk down the stairs, and when I returned to my office, Lattice was already there.

Lattice has been waiting for Spasimo to leave. He throws me hard against the wall of the hallway and then ties me with a hiking rope to the leather arm chair where others usually sit, leaving behind fibers, traces, sweat...

He says he won't hurt me if I just listen to him, because since the day when Donatella went away, he hasn't had any peace. I agree with him, wary of his intentions. ("Weren't you the one who uncovered my wife's affairs and told me about them on the telephone? What tact, Mrs. Cantini, what tact...")

They had been drinking, he and his poker buddies, and they wanted to scare her, so she would stop humiliating him and maybe even mend her ways. After giving her a few slaps, his friends kept their distance and slipped away when he signaled to them with a snap of his fingers. He controls them through blackmail, but one of them by now is certainly talking to the homicide detectives, telling them how it happened. He has no way to escape and knows it; he's been in jail; this time they'll give him life in prison. He's anxious to tell me what he thought as he strangled his wife: "You're either with me or no one." ("But revenge, my dear, isn't all pure pleasure..."). So he's decided to put an end to it: he'll jump from my office window, which is right on the fifth floor. He'll die on the spot, he says, and in the meantime he lifts the shutter. (Do I want to follow him? Go away with him?)

I haven't struggled, and he hasn't tied the rope too tight. I'm scared, but not terrified. The only thing I don't want is to help him fly and hit the ground below. I summon up all my cynicism and speak to him as they do on TV: "Listen to me, Lattice. You're a wounded man..."

"Do you feel sorry for me?"

"It's obvious you didn't know what you were doing. You let your hand take over."

"Bullshit."

"If you untie me, I'll show you something."

"What?"

"A Beretta."

"Why?"

"Take this rope off."

"You think I'm an idiot?"

"I just want to give you a weapon that you can use away from here."

He nods. Impassive. Disoriented.

"If you put it in your mouth or point it at your heart or your temple, wherever you prefer, it will be faster and less painful than leaping into the void, believe me. If you do it from the fifth floor, there's a risk you'll live. But crippled."

He sneers. "I don't believe you." Meanwhile he opens all the desk drawers.

"Have you ever fired a gun?"

He doesn't answer me.

"I'll explain how to do it. Come on, take this rope off me."

He hesitates, then sweeps up everything and throws it into the air — pens, notebooks, photos, documents, even *The Young Detective's Handbook* by Mario Nardone, my personal bible.

"Listen," I insist, "your life means nothing to me. You're free to do what you want with it, but I don't want to see your blood out front and have to remember it every time I come into the agency. Take the Beretta and go shoot yourself wherever you like — on the bus, in the park, at your house. This will be your way to pay me for my work. A bill you still haven't settled, remember?"

He examines me, dumbfounded. "You're cold-blooded, Mrs. Cantini."

(I'd like to tell him no, I'm not. I'm shitting in my pants.) "I got it from my father."

He opens the window. "Are you really that attached to your agency?"

"Yes, and I'd rather it not be involved."

Then he closes it.

Giordano Lattice comes slowly toward me and frees me from the rope without saying anything. As I massage my chafed wrists, he orders me to hand over the weapon.

I look at him. "I'm terribly sorry, Lattice. I've never had a gun, and I never will."

Whatever he'll say or do now is a mystery. I stand in front of him and look at the ground, sincerely unhappy about not being able to honor our agreement. The silence is tense, and I'm almost paralyzed, incapable of running out of the room or screaming like a crazy woman. The only thing I can do is brush my pants, as if I had spotted a hair or a small stain. I don't know why, but Lattice must find this situation comic. He suddenly bursts into asthmatic laughter, curling up on the floor with his back against the wall and the hiking rope twisted in his hands. His polenta-yellow hair looks like a nest of canaries flattened on the white wall. And it's then that I move instinctively in front of the window with my arms wide open: "No one leaves from here." Lattice continues to laugh like a madman even when I grab the phone. Fifteen minutes later, I hand over a live killer to Luca Bruni.

It's almost dark when I call Spasimo on the cell phone and tell him what he missed out on. He can't believe it. He never goes out at that hour, and what do you know, all hell breaks loose as soon as he leaves for a dentist appointment. Finally, he gets serious. "What if he had hurt you? What if he had pushed you out the window?"

"Oh," I tease him, "you would never have forgiven me."

We tell each other some more crap before saying goodbye, stuff like I'll be away for a while, yes, it's a little vacation. I deserve a break from the agency and its headaches. Then there's my father. It's time for him to be boss again. That way, he'd be distracted and maybe, you know, drink less. Me too, but don't even think about getting rid of me. I'll invite you to dinner one of these evenings. Yes, all right, I'll pay more attention to the menu. You still have to tell me about the night you spent with your colleague from Sacramento. I want to know all about it. You thought I had forgotten? There's a chance we'll become friends, Lucio. Genuine friends.

I leave the agency and find myself beneath a rainy, electric-blue sky. I don't have running shoes on, but I run all the same, and when I get into the car, water cascades from my face and hair, and I shiver in every part of my body.

I drive through the lights of a city that is emerging from its offices, bars, stores, and entrance ways, crowding under its porticos and quickening its step, jumping over puddles. On the back seat, there's still a shoe box full of Ada's letters, including the last one, dated January 31, which contains these words among so many others:

I never wonder why Mama did it. That gesture came to her from afar like a sound or a color, and not in the form of a thought. She simply had to do it, like the things you do and don't see yourself doing while you do them. She had lost awareness of herself, and she was somewhere else, like something that had never even existed. If she had thought about us, perhaps she wouldn't have done it. But killing yourself is a rejection that encompasses everything and everybody...

I drape a cloth over the box, as if to protect it from gusts of wind or hide it from the curious gaze of the world.

We are all bottomless wells, that's what I think: Me, my sister, my mother, my father, Andrea Berti, Spasimo, my clients, everyone, one and all. Bottomless wells. As hard as I try, as much as I rack my brains, as many free interpretations as I make...

I watch people hurry along the pedestrian crossings, under the leaden sky, under a tireless rain. We all turn into mud, Gaia would say if she were here with me.

My sister also passes by, faintly, over those stripes. She turns her eyes, those gray-blue orbs of hers, with the same giddiness she had at the piano, immersed in the harmonies, in the middle of our old living room. I hear her play Grieg with an expression of ecstasy. "I'm sleepy," she says, as she abruptly

closes the instrument. Then she gets up, goes down the narrow
hallway, climbs the stairs, and shuts herself in our room. I look
at the book by Pascal spread open on my knees and underline
in pencil: "Love, abandoning the solitude of the hateful me,
accepts the great void." I have to talk about this with Ada, I
tell myself. Yes, she can explain what it means. I go upstairs. I
enter the room. I sit on her bed and watch her sleep.

I open my eyes and brake suddenly. No, I haven't crashed
into anyone.

I open the car window and let in a blast of wind mixed with
rain. I turn around. The shoe box has fallen from the seat. The
wind is displacing the pages, scattering them on the floor. An
envelope is stuck between the gas pedal and my foot.

I stop the car along a lane lined with chestnut trees because
I don't see anyone, only my sister who studies me with childish
seriousness. I collapse against the steering wheel, seized by a
sense of abandonment. I relax the muscles of my face and
realize that it's sopping wet. I look around, and everything is
blurry. I simply weep.

I get out of the Citroën and go into the first bar I find. I
order a gin bitter. I drink it in three seconds and climb back
in the car.

Dear Ada,

*This time I'm writing you a letter, even if, between the two of us,
I wasn't the one who used to write. I write it mentally, between
one traffic light and the next, so forgive me if it doesn't amount to
much. It's just that I'm thinking how much I missed your sounds
in the room when you left. It's been hard, Ada, losing those sounds.
Yes, you ought to know it…*

*I live in an apartment you wouldn't like, that you'd describe
as kitsch, with the shutters always closed, and objects and clothes
strewn on the floor. There's a photo of you in almost every room,
because there are times I don't remember what you were like, and
then I look for you in these photos, even if they're never faithful. The*

only thing you'd like about my place is the little terrace cluttered with vases of flowers and plants, which I never have time to water and almost all of which die right in front of me (I wonder why). As you see, I haven't taken after Mama. I'd be happy if I could tell you that we'll see each again someday. Fuck, it would be fantastic.

The problem is that, as hard as I try, I don't believe it.

The problem, Ada, is that there's a fire in my belly, and it's fueled by alcohol, because I've got to have something to hold on to.

The problem is that I hope there's an epic poem on the theme of fragility, otherwise, I have no excuses. The problem is that I'm bruised, worn out, crushed, like everyone else.

The problem, Ada, is that life is a lot worse than we imagined it at fifteen. The problem is that the emotions I feel, for myself and for other people, are intermittent. The problem is that you're not a dossier, you're not one of my cases, and there's no sign, no indication, nothing, to help me solve it. The problem is that, even if I've lost the habit of loving my fellow human beings, I still believe that loving each other, burying each other, drinking a beer together, are the most important things that can happen to us.

The problem, Ada, is that I'll never stop missing you.

But the great thing, you know, because it's a wonderful thing after all, is that your smell is unmistakable, and if I put my nose in a place where you've been, I get some sense of direction…

I keep driving. I notice an argument between a father and his adolescent daughter in front of the entrance to a building. Then my eyes shift toward him. He's set a small cage on the counter of the Dog & Cat Store and is talking with Patty. I note the fingers of the sales girl as she caresses the cat through the bars. After a few minutes, I see him leave the store holding the cage with one hand and a bag of tin cans with the other. He crosses the street, and I bend my head so he won't see me. When I hear a hand knock on the window, I rub my inflamed right eye. I lift my head. I look at A. on the other side of the glass. Then I drive away.

◉⊙◉

This Book Was Completed on December 1, 2017

At Italica Press, New York, New York.

It Was Set in Garamond and

Garamond Expert.

Lightning Source UK Ltd.
Milton Keynes UK
UKHW012245161221
395788UK00002B/537